P.D. HAYNIE

Storybook Orc

Spiral Path

Publications

First published by Spiral Path Publications 2020

Copyright © 2020 by P.D. Haynie

This novel is entirely a work of fiction. The names, characters and incidents portrayed in it are the work of the author's imagination. Any resemblance to actual persons, living or dead, events or localities is entirely coincidental.

P.D. Haynie asserts the moral right to be identified as the author of this work.

The world of Grandilar, and the various unique places, persons, creatures, and organizations of the "Dragon Storm" game are used under license from Gatekeeper Publishing. (Iteration 082020)

First edition

ISBN: 978-1-950237-11-1

This book was professionally typeset on Reedsy.
Find out more at reedsy.com

For anyone who has ever walked the surface of Grandilar, and seen a Warp Storm on the horizon.

Contents

Preface

Somewhere I got it into my head that a sufficiently talented fantasy writer shouldn't need an expository preface to enable his readers to make sense of his story. It was a silly idea, and I have no idea where it came from; Tolkien felt that *The Lord of the Rings* needed an expository preface, and while I am seldom accused of having great wisdom, I certainly know better than to attack the credentials of JRRT.

This story stands pretty well on its own, but it was originally written for an audience that was already familiar with the setting. As I am now attempting to broaden that audience, some sort of introduction seems necessary.

I first encountered Susan Van Camp's *Dragon Storm* game sometime in 1996, in the form of a bright orange card box with a roaring green dragon on the front. The back of the box described a card based role playing game (still a pretty unusual concept two decades later) in which players became shape-shifting freedom fighters (Dwarven Gargoyles, Elven Unicorns, Human Dragons and Werewolves) in a world controlled by evil necromancers. I was intrigued. I was also broke, and in the game store for a specific item for which I had saved (the identity of which has been lost to time). I sadly put the box back on the shelf.

A year and a change in financial circumstances later, I finally bought one of those little orange boxes. The cards were beautiful, the game mechanics were decent, if a bit simple for my rather masochistic tastes, and the setting…

I fell head over heels in love with the world. It was a beautiful and magical place in which the bad guys had WON. The player characters had amazing gifts with which to fight their soul-eating enemies, but those very gifts also made them targets. And on top of that, since the enemy was in control, the common people believed that the shape-shifters were WORSE than the ruling necromancers. The shape-shifters supposedly controlled the huge magical "dragon" storms that shredded the landscape and caused horrible mutations in anyone unfortunate enough to get caught in one. Of course, there was always a chance that someone who had a bit of dragon's blood in them might find themselves changed into a shape-shifter by the storm, and since dragons had ruled the world for thousands of years, and could shape-shift, and... Let's just say that EVERYONE had a drop or two of dragon's blood. Things could get complicated.

While the dragons had ruled the world for thousands of years, that changed some two hundred years before my story starts. During a draconic religious festival in which all of the most powerful dragons were in deep trance states (The Day of the Dead, or "Death Day"), a coalition of draconic enemies attacked and killed the sleeping dragons and stole their power, releasing enormous amounts of toxic magical "warp" into the world in the process. The triumphant coalition then dissolved into a back stabbing brawl, but the damage was done. The ancient dragons were dead, and the warp using necromancers were in control.

World-designer Van Camp calls the world "Grandilar" and has given most of the traditional fantasy races a bit of a twist. Grandilar's orcs are light-fingered gray-skinned wanderers who revere dragons, worship their ancestors, and enjoy causing trouble, but are not fundamentally malevolent. Dwarves have a predilection for stone and metal work, but have been so scattered by wars with dragons, necromancers, and each other that they have no culture of their own. Elves are long lived and magical, and their heritage is in the forests, but only the dark skinned Ebony elves have maintained their original culture. The fair-skinned Farillan elves have been assimilated into the general mortal polyglot culture, and the warped (and often green skinned) Haskalads are both the leaders and the primary victims of the necromantic regime. Humans, as usual, are a little bit of everything. And that is only the major races; there are the wakana man-wolves, werewolves who sacrificed the power to shift shape to warp magic; the vermite rat people; deer— and goat— and sheep— headed Vorn, who tend to eat their enemies; the Tigreans (anthropomorphic tigers); the Das Karr (anthropomorphic foxes, occasionally with wings); ghosts of every size and temperament; the list goes on.

And then there is the matter of religion... The dragons never seemed to feel a need for religion, but the mortals in their service chose to worship an earth goddess named Elethay. When the necromancers came to power, they invented an alternative goddess named Jikadell, and it seems likely that after a couple of hundred years of insincere worship, there just might be a person behind the name after all. And then there is Valaria, the raven haired barbarian werewolf who, five hundred years before my story starts, jumped into the middle of a bonfire and predicted a day when the dragons would be brought low, and evil beyond imagining would walk the world. When she stepped out of the fire, Valaria found that her hair had turned permanently red. She soon learned that there was no way to avoid the coming cataclysm, and started training people to survive and fight back in a world that the dragons no longer ruled. Valaria died before the Death Day massacre, but her legacy lives on in the "Valarian Champions", one of the few forces for good in the otherwise bleak landscape of Grandilar.

And having said that, on with the story.

P.D. Haynie

Acknowledgement

To Susan Van Camp, who built the world;

To Mark Harmon, who designed the game;

To Tim Kennard, who kept the lights on;

And to Jim Keeley, who opened the door.

This book simply would not have exited without all of you. Thanks.

P.D. Haynie

Prologue: Willow

Willow reached the end of the row she was weeding, stood up, and stretched. She looked across the river to the west and squinted at the advancing clouds that had blocked the late afternoon sun before it could settle behind the forest. A storm, definitely, though at this range she still could not tell if the advancing clouds signaled a natural storm or something more sinister. She decided she had time to weed at least one more row and turned to her task.

She hoped that it would just be rain; any sane person would, of course. She wasted a happy moment at the thought of standing in the cold rain and letting it run over her, and of pulling a comb through her hair as the water poured through it. "I ought to hate rain," she thought, but knew better. Nature's rain had not burned rivulets of scar tissue into her skin; the Dragon's rain had done that.

She finished another row and looked across the river to gauge the progress of the storm. There was still time for at least one more row, and she was still unsure if nature or dragons drove the storm. Willow dropped her gaze from sky to forest, and sighed sadly. If only…

If only what? All of her life, those woods had meant freedom to Willow, freedom from a life where no one valued her as anything other than a field hand and a joke topic. She was known as the tallest man, the ugliest man, and the hardest-working man in the village, that she was not a man at all not withstanding. Across the river (assuming she could make the swim, which was doubtful) there were no chores, no villagers, no Haskalad overseers... no certain food, and no shelter. But there was freedom.

Another row finished, Willow stood to check the progress of the storm and gasped in horror. The storm front was galloping across the river in red and blue draconic fury at the speed of a fast horse. Willow wasted a quick glance toward the village—impossible minutes away even at a dead run-and charged straight into the storm. If she could submerge herself in the river, she might avoid the worst of the storm's hostile magic. She closed her eyes as she hit the storm front, hoping that the rain would not be too hostile. Dragon's rain could be anything: boiling hot, freezing cold, acidic, mud laden; it almost always carried the magical disease called the Tox.

She had one foot on the riverbank when the lightning struck her, and then she was in the water and impossibly tangled in her clothing and her limbs didn't seem to be working properly. Her face broke the surface, and she watched herself gulp air through the long snout...

She had been transformed into a wolf! She was a shape-shifter! Willow took a deep breath and allowed herself to sink while she tore free of the remains of her clothing, an easy task now that she knew what limbs she was working with. That done, she returned to the surface and swam resolutely toward the west bank of the river, and freedom.

One: The Blank Slate

It is said that once upon a time, before the dragons had learned to shape-shift, they decided to use their magics to create a race of perfect servitors. The creatures they created were strong, and quick, and prolific, and so hardy that they could live on a diet of filth and poison.

Unfortunately, they used their own criminals and lunatics as raw material, and the creatures were invariably surly, uncooperative, and not quite sane.

The dragons called them, "Orcs".

—Leod, the Storyteller of Freepost

I woke up in a pleasant forest meadow. The sun was warm, the grass was cool, and the birds were singing sweetly. I felt like the local militia had used my body as a drill field while breaking in their new hob-nailed boots. I opened the eye that wasn't buried in the turf and saw nothing of consequence, so I gritted my teeth and lifted my head to have a look around. The birds stopped singing. After I had forced my unhappy body into a sitting position, I was still in a pleasant forest meadow. I was also stark naked and hopelessly lost.

I found myself staring at my hand, which was the color of mildewed rawhide— not a color I normally associated with living tissue. I looked closer and saw vestigial scales, which meant I was an orc. I didn't remember being an orc. On the other hand, I didn't honestly remember NOT being an orc...

Orcdom was not a bad state, all things considered. Orcs could thrive on a diet of anything their teeth could grind, and their teeth could grind anything of animal or vegetable origin. I found a likely looking tree, and set about gnawing it off at the base. Several hours of boredom later, I had a very serviceable spear with a bit of a hook on its nether end. I climbed into a tree to watch the sun set and try to sleep; my spear was tangled with a nearby branch and within easy reach.

I didn't have a name. I'm tempted to say I knew nothing about myself, but that would not be true; I knew I was well educated. I could name the titles of several books I had read, and I could recite most of "The Fall of Aneshka Skyrider," but I had no context for the knowledge; I knew that literacy was unusual because I had read the fact in a book.

I assumed that I had been teleported into the clearing where I awakened; I was no tracker, but the earth was soft and there were no marks of any kind except those I had made myself. As far as I knew, I couldn't cast a teleport spell, and there was no way to teleport someone without going oneself— or so my books told me. So someone had taken me out here and left me, which meant I had a fairly powerful enemy. No name, but an enemy. Such joy!

I had an odd feeling that I didn't belong in my body, as if it were a new set of clothes that were not quite broken in. I had no idea if that were meaningful or not; there were too many things definitely wrong with my mind to make much of a vague uneasiness. The sun went down; I relaxed into my tree branch, and fell asleep.

The next day I started marching in a direction that approximated north. That is, I intended to keep the sun to my right until it was fairly high in the sky, and then head straight for the sun until it was definitely descending, and then keep it to my leftt. I wouldn't travel straight, but I WOULD end up farther north than I started...

It was roughly noon when I came to a rather large meadow and started across it; my feet were holding up well, and I felt as good about my situation as I sanely could. And then suddenly something sharp hit me in the back and knocked me head over heels; I managed to hold onto the spear by instinct. There was a sensation in my shoulders that I knew was going to be pain in a few seconds, and I suspected that I had been cut— or torn— badly. I forced myself to my feet and pivoted, looking for the source of my injury.

Something vaguely draconic was diving straight at me; I hurled myself out of the way, and thrust the spear into its belly as I ducked. The spear cut; the creature's claws didn't. I stood again and got ready for the next pass.

I watched it turn, and recognized it as a gilga spawn, a warp creature, rather than a dragon. Not as smart as a dragon— or an orc, for that matter— but still much better armed and armored than I was. It tried another flying grab, and again I managed to hit it on the dodge.

It didn't learn; it tried the same trick five more times, and each time I hurt it a little bit more. On the last pass I managed to rip open one of its wings, and it crashed to the ground in a heap. It rolled back onto its feet, though, and spun around angrily, looking for its prey.

I was spent; the tension and the blood loss had taken their toll. I faced the monster unsteadily, and hoped it would impale itself on my spear; I was exhausted and out of tricks. The gilga came in low, mouth agape; I shifted the spear butt from my right instep to my right hand, and shoved the spear into the gilga's mouth; I think it was already dead when it barreled into me, but I still ended up underneath it.

Once the shock of being alive wore off, I wormed my way free, and had a truly disgusting meal of raw gilga breast. My books told me that orcs could eat warp tainted meat without ill effect, but my throat didn't seem to understand that very well. Still, it couldn't have been much worse than the cellulose I had eaten the day before. I found a respectable tree and hauled myself into it, and then waited to either heal or die.

I didn't move the next day, but by dawn of the day after that I was ready for another meal of gilga meat, and continued walking. Eventually I came to a decent sized watercourse, and I followed THAT downstream until it brought me to an obviously navigable river, and I followed that downstream as well, because otherwise I would have had to swim. Five days after my fight with the gilga I found myself on the edge of civilization.

The edge of civilization, in this case, consisted of a horned elf, a wakana wolf-man, and an orc arguing over who was going get the first chance to rape the vermite rat-girl they had captured. They didn't notice me as I approached.

I stopped and thought about it. The gilga wounds on my back were no longer fresh, but a long way from fully healed. And there were three of them, and they had real weapons, and all I had was a pointy stick. I would be an idiot to interfere...

...Except that I had a head full of heroic poetry, and that I was painfully aware that I had NO other ethical decisions in my memory. I was a blank slate, and the next few moments were going to determine what kind of character I had, if any.

"Let the girl go, boys," I said, with as much conviction as I could muster. The trio looked up, gaped, and started to laugh. "I am quite serious," I continued; once you start to bluff, you have to play it through. "Let her go, or die."

The elf scowled, caught the wakana's eye, and jerked his thumb at me. The wakana drew his sword and advanced. I dodged the wakana's sword and managed to crease his hide a bit with my spear. The wakana growled; the elf said, "Hold her," presumably to the orc, and drew his own sword; I started to back away.

They tried to surround me, which is difficult with only two men. It forced them to separate enough that I was able to charge in for a quick exchange of blows with the elf before the wakana could get involved. My blow landed; the elf's didn't, and then I was off again. They didn't change their tactics, and I managed to deliver a butt stroke to the elf's face that took him down.

I turned to face the Wakana, and managed to hit him again while his sword whistled past my shoulder; I hit him a third time, and felt his sword bite into me. We separated, and I missed my footing; I was set to feel that sword a second time when I realized that my wild thrust had caught the wakana high in the belly, and that his next blow would never fall.

I recovered my spear, and made my way back to the orc and his prisoner; my fight with Brother Orc's companions had taken us a fair distance away. I found Brother Orc hitching up his trousers; he had apparently taken my intervention as an opportunity to move to the head of the line with regard to the vermite girl. I would have spitted him where he stood, but he heard me coming and dove for his spear.

I stabbed him, dodged his return, and stabbed him again. I mistimed the next dodge, and took a solid thrust to the leg in penalty. We separated, then closed again, and I managed to land the killing blow before he could hit me again. I settled wearily to my knees.

After I had caught my breath, I looked at the vermite girl, who was watching me through tear filled eyes while she clutched at the remains of her clothing. "Do you know your way home from here?" I asked quietly; she nodded once, slowly. "Then go home." She shook her head; I sighed, and got to my feet. "Follow me, then," I said.

I planted my spear in the dirt, then recovered Brother Orc's spear and planted it as well. I took a few deep breaths, then hoisted Brother Orc onto my shoulder, grabbed his spear, and walked to where I had left the bodies of the elf and the wakana. I cut all three throats with the elf's dagger (just to be sure), then stripped the elf and the orc; I had no interest in the wakana's fetid loincloth, but I did take his swordbelt and his purse. That done, I bundled my new possessions and carried them to the river, where I washed the clothing as thoroughly as I could. The girl followed and watched me with wide eyes.

The elf's clothes were of much better quality, but the orc's fit. I offered the elf's shirt to the girl; she took it, and put it on. The clothes were soggy, but the day was warm, and it felt good to actually have clothing again. The girl seemed to agree. I strapped on the elf's sword and dagger, tied the elf's buckler to the wakana's swordbelt with the elf's trousers and slung THAT over my shoulder, then picked up the orc's spear.

"Can you still find your way home?" I asked the girl; she nodded again. "Do you have a name?"

"Pepper." she said so quietly I could barely hear.

"Well, then, Pepper, unless you have a better idea, we might as well go there. I not only don't have a home, I don't even have a name."

That startled her. "No name? How can you not have a name?"

I shrugged, and it hurt; everything hurt. "I have no idea. I woke up in a meadow a few days ago; I have a head full of history books, but no idea who I am or how I got there." Pepper shook her head doubtfully, then turned and started walking; I followed her.

The sun was setting when we arrived at the edge of a small village; I could see the lights of a much larger town across the river. The village consisted of a vermite warren and a few more substantial buildings, the largest of which was farthest away, and had the look of a smithy. At the edge of the warren I was suddenly surrounded by a wary crowd of vermites, and Pepper was nowhere to be seen. I planted the butt of my spear and leaned on it heavily, wondering what would happen next.

I didn't have long to wait; a one-legged dwarf with the shoulders of a pack horse hobbled out of the growing darkness. He looked me over with interest.

"Three of them, you say?" the dwarf asked no one in particular, then looked me in the eye.

"Take off your shirt, boy." I shrugged and did as I was told. "That sword cut is going to need a fair amount of sewing, boy. And where did the claw marks come from?"

"Gilga spawn. Five days ago."

"They could use some work, too... That blood on your trousers yours?"

I nodded. "This spear. Previous owner." Some of the vermites snickered at that, but the dwarf didn't even smile.

"You outran a gilga spawn, boy?"

I shook my head. "Killed it. It only hit me the once; that was enough."

"With your teeth?"

I shook my head again. "Wooden spear that I made with my teeth, and sharpened against a rock. Same one I used today."

9

"So where'd you leave it?"

"Stuck in the ground, where I left it after I got this one." I jostled my spear indicatively.

The dwarf stared into my face for a long moment, then said, "There's a place in the forge where you can sleep tonight. In the morning we'll look into having those wounds treated, if you live that long." He turned and stumped off toward the smithy; I followed him. He wasn't fast on his peg leg, but I wasn't very fast, either.

It felt odd to stretch out flat and sleep under a roof for the first time. I was sure that I must have done so before, but... that was before. That was in the life that seemed to be lost.

There was a noise at the smithy door, then it opened and Pepper came in carrying a blanket. She gave it to me, and stared at me for several seconds. "I prayed to the Red Lady," she said, so softly I could barely hear her even in the stillness. "I prayed to Elethay the Warrior that you would come back and kill him, and you did. Thank you."

I wrapped myself in the blanket. "Thank the Lady," I said. "And you're welcome. Thank you for the blanket." I think she smiled at that, then she turned and left.

I dreamed that night...

I dreamed that I was in a large, dark room, and that something was pounding on what I knew was the door. The door burst open, and a dragon entered. The dragon had an aura of size, and power, and majesty, though it did not actually seem to take up very much space. It looked straight at me for a very long time, and then I felt it smile, though its face did not move.

The room got brighter, and I could see that the walls were lined with books on bookshelves. The dragon took a book off the shelf, and opened it, and seemed surprised by what it saw. It replaced that book, and looked at another, and then a third, and then it looked at me some more. It seemed pleased.

At the far side of the room there was a large door that was locked and barred; the dragon went to it, looked at me again, and then tore the door off of its hinges. There was an air of wrongness in the room, in addition to another dragon which had an aura of being weak and confused and afraid, even though it looked a great deal like the first dragon. The weak dragon was guarding a pile of debris which contained the bones of an elf and several shredded books.

The first dragon looked at me, and again I felt it smile, then it turned and flew away. I turned to look for the second dragon, but it was gone, and I was standing on the pile of shredded books. I sat down, and the dream ended.

The dwarf returned at dawn; he was carrying my wooden spear, and using it as a staff. He dressed my wounds personally, and I thought that he was also casting healing magic as he did so. After he was finished, he sat on a box and offered me his hand. "Perrin Ironhand," he said; I shook his hand.

"I would tell you my name, " I began.

"But you don't have one. I know. One will find you, I think. Are you looking for work, or just passing through?"

"I have no idea," I answered. "Is there work to be found?"

"I could stand another apprentice, if you don't mind hard work."

"I could do with some food and a softer bed…"

Perrin laughed. "I imagine you could. I can arrange it."

"Then I guess you have an apprentice."

"Well enough. Welcome to Ferrypoint." And we shook hands again.

Two: Names and Places

In this town the two temples stand right across the street from each other, and you'll hear pretty much the same song on either side. The Jikadell priestesses will tell you that the dragons and other shapshifters send the storms, and that the various mutations that the storms cause are gifts of Jikadell, even if they drive you mad. The Elethay priestesses will tell you that Jikadell's necromancers cause the storms, and that if a storm happens to turn you into a shape shifter, that is a gift of Elethay.

Which side do I believe? Let me give you a clue.

When Elethay's junior priestesses aren't in the temple studying, they're out in the wild hunting madspawn.

When Jikadell's junior priestesses aren't turning tricks for cash, they're locked in the basement.

—Leod, the Storyteller of Freepost

"First thing you need to do, " Perrin said, "Is lose those clothes. Their owner probably has friends, and they might recognize the clothes or the weapons. Of course, I could refit and re-temper the blades…"

"For a small fee," I responded with a grin; a dwarf is a dwarf, after all.

Perrin grinned back. "I just want to break even. How about I give you a sword for a sword, a dagger for a dagger, and so on; I'll keep the second sword for my trouble, and give you 50 Imperials in change. Sound fair? With their purses, you should have a fair start. You DID grab their purses, didn't you?"

I grinned again, and nodded. "It sounds more than fair."

"Good. Hate to think you were stupid." He started to gather the weapons that had briefly been mine. "Talk to Jasmine at the store; she'll take care of you. And take today to get your bearings; I'll put you to work first thing tomorrow." He stumped away, and I gathered up my blanket.

Jasmine turned out to be short, round and extremely pleasant; she was ever so slightly too tall and fine boned to be a dwarf, but it was a VERY near thing. I selected weapons and clothing, lusted briefly over a greatsword that was far out of my price range, and bought a tinderbox and a blanket of my own.

"I don't suppose you have any names for sale, do you?" I asked, and Jasmine just grinned and shook her head; she apparently knew my story already. "Have to ask, you know. Could you tell me where we are?"

Jasmine looked at me curiously, then said, "The city across the river is Lechmoor; the river is the Boggy. Does that help?"

I thought about it and shook my head. "Not so far. Keep going from there."

"Something bigger than the river? This is the East Branch of the Kanchaka valley…"

"Kanchaka! That's a name I've heard. Isn't that where Valaria the Heretic came from?"

Jasmine looked at me a bit oddly, but I was too excited to worry about it. "I think so, yes," she said slowly.

"Can I waste a pinch of your flour?" I asked as I reached for the barrel; Jasmine nodded vaguely. I took a bit of flour and dusted the countertop, then marked off a rectangle. "This is north, and there is the ocean along the east edge, and this section in the north east is the warp elf Haskalad Empire, and this down here is the dark elf Celestial Empire. And these," I drew a line down the center of my map, "Are the Chiseled Mountains, and up here in the northwest is Kanchaka Valley!"

Jasmine didn't lose her puzzled expression. "And where is home, then?"

I stared at my map, and my face fell, then I started to laugh. "I have no idea whatsoever. Somewhere in one of the empires, though; every map I can remember centers on one or the other. And I can remember several city maps... Perhaps I moved around a great deal?"

Jasmine wiped the counter and dusted it again. She drew an oval and indicated that its major axis was north/south. "This is Kanchaka valley." She drew a line from the top to the center. "Blighted Ridge, and this is Goldentooth in the center. " She finished the line from top to bottom, then added two more to divide the map into six more-or-less equal wedges. "You can worry about the rest of the geography some other time; this is the political map. Starting here," she indicated the northeast wedge, "Lechmoor district is Haskalad, but loose. This side of the river, Perrin is pretty much the only law, and we like it that way.

"This next wedge is solid Haskalad. There are two cities: New Mercer, which is a sort of freehold under a madman named Brickwall, and Bogtown, which is the local Haskalad capitol, seat of Duke Stygius Nemesis, known to most folks as Black Bane.

"The next wedge is run by raptors, but tributary to the Empire, which makes it uncomfortable for just about everyone, and the next wedge is run by raptors who are NOT tributary to the Empire, which makes the border REALLY interesting. Up here in the northwest there is a good-sized Ebony Elf enclave.

"And in between... Well, there's a dragon clan called the Zachtos who claim the whole valley, and actually have some power here, and there are the last remains of the old Manilac Kingdom. That's where Valaria got her start, and she still has plenty of followers in the area. And plenty of low rent necromancers hunting them."

I was vaguely aware that Jasmine had kept her eyes on my face the entire time was talking. I looked up and met her gaze. "Are you expecting me to take sides? I'm Perrin's apprentice; I'll follow his lead unless I have good reason not to."

Jasmine shook her head and smiled slightly. "It's really all gone, isn't it? You have no idea who you were?"

"No, I don't. You sound as if you do, though."

"I only know what Ravin told us," Jasmine answered.

"And who is Ravin, and what does he know about me?" I was beginning to get angry, but I kept it in check; I could see that Jasmine wasn't trying to goad me, she was just being cautious.

"I thought Perrin was going to tell you; I don't think I should..."

I swallowed my anger. "Please Jasmine. I need to know."

Jasmine looked me in the eyes. "Ravin is a dead dragon..." She waited for me to react, and I shrugged. "He visited you, last night, to see if we could trust you."

"And he told you something that confused you?"

"He said that you were honest, and decent, but that you used to be a necromancer yourself. And that you were once an elf, probably Ebonese." She stopped, still waiting for my reaction; since her words didn't contradict anything I knew, I didn't react at all. "He also said that you were extremely well educated, and that you were a dragon."

I don't know what reaction Jasmine was looking for; I doubt that she was disappointed; I didn't quite fall over.

"Ravin also thinks that when the Dragon within you awoke, it somehow killed the original you, the part of you that was a necromancer." Jasmine kept looking at me for confirmation; I shook my head to clear it, then shrugged again.

"It makes as much sense as anything. The good news is that you are potentially immortal. The bad news is that everyone hates you, and there is a price on your head.'" I looked into Jasmine's eyes. "But you don't feel that way, and Perrin doesn't." Jasmine didn't respond. "Kindred spirits, perhaps?" Jasmine smiled at that, but said nothing.

I looked down at my purchases, and compared the blanket I had just bought to the one I had slept under. I pushed the newer blanket toward Jasmine. "Could you see that this gets to Pepper the vermite? I like to return better than I borrow."

Jasmine smiled at that, then looked at the dust map on the counter and snapped her fingers. She reached under the counter and pulled out a wooden box. "Just the thing for the orc of letters," she said.

The box contained a well-sealed inkwell, several pieces of parchment, and a number of quills. I tried to keep the lust out of my eyes as I asked, "And the price?"

"Thirty-five, but I can give you some credit if you need it, and promise to never tell anyone I did it." She was grinning as she said it.

I counted out the coins. "Done. And I don't need credit at the moment; brigand bashing seems to pay fairly well." Jasmine took my money with a smile, and I went off to stow my belongings.

Noon found me sitting on a large rock on the riverbank, enjoying the sun, and starting a journal. I heard a group of people approaching, and put my quill behind my ear; I looked up to see five soldiers approaching me.

They had to be soldiers, in spite of their different races; there was something distinctly military about every move they made. They were led by an elf with bat's wings and a magnificent pair of ram's horns; I put away my ink and parchment as smoothly as possible.

"Groundley," the leader said, "Have I ever killed an orc?"

"No, master," replied the only human in the group.

"Well, let's correct that, shall we?" The elf drew his sword, and I prepared to be where his sword wasn't.

"You might want to ask my permission before you carve up my apprentice," Perrin called; I flicked my eyes away from the elf long enough to see

18

that Perrin, Jasmine, several vermites, and a few others were all pointing crossbows at my erstwhile companions. "If you have a grievance, challenge him, or take it to court."

The elf looked around, weighed the odds, and sheathed his sword. "Very well then," he said to me. "I challenge you, for the offense of being an orc, and being ugly, and being in my line of sight." He turned to Perrin. "NOW can I kill him?"

"Orc?" Perrin called.

I looked at the elf. "Cudgels. No armor. No flight, no horns, no magic. Now." I said as clearly as I could.

The elf looked from me to Perrin and back in frustration, then said, "Very well. Done."

I took off my shirt and accepted the cudgel that Perrin gave me; he grinned at me. He also managed to get the elf and his companions to wager against me at three to one odds; I wasn't sure how I felt about that.

Perrin signaled the start; I landed a solid blow, and managed to dodge the first of a three-strike salvo the elf threw in return. I struck again, and again was repaid three to one, with two landing. I was hurt, and worried, but the elf was completely out of tricks; his seventh blow was so easy to dodge it barely existed, and I hit him solidly a third time.

He cheated. He came at me with his horns, and I countered; I realized I was wide open to his cudgel, then watched it fall from his hand just before he hit the turf. I stood up stiffly; the elf's companions dragged him back to the ferry.

Perrin was grinning broadly as he gathered his winnings; I scowled at him as I picked up my shirt. "Oh, so the feathered orc would have rather

LOST?" he laughed.

"Feathered?" I asked; Perrin pulled my pen from behind my ear and waved it at me.

"You ever seen a quilla snake, boy?" he asked; I shook my head. "Folks, we have here a literate orc who moves like a snake. I think we're going to call him Quill." He gave my pen back to me with a flourish and a hint of a bow. I accepted the pen and thought about it; I could do worse, and the gallery seemed to approve. I offered Perrin my hand for the third time that morning, and he responded by handing me a bag of coins. "Your cut. Should make the bruises hurt less."

I stared at him dumbfounded as he stumped away, then put on my shirt, recovered my writing kit, and resumed my journal.

The sun was well in the west when I wandered over to the odd-looking raft that gave Ferrypoint its name. There was a chest-high windlass in the center of the northern edge of the raft which carried a chain that ran across the river to a short pier on either side. The operator was sitting with his back against the windlass frame, absently throwing stones into the river. As I got closer I realized that he was a vermite, and easily the biggest vermite I had ever seen; he was as tall as any and built like a STOUT treestump.

"What does a crossing cost?" I asked.

"Two. Three for a round trip, same day, in advance. Ten for a horse, fifty for a wagon. You're free, though."

"Oh? And why would I ride free?"

"Pepper is my sister. I'm Tobacco; folks call me 'Bacco." He extended an enormous hand, and I took it; I was a little surprised that I was most of a

20

head taller than he was, though he must have been twice my weight.

"I guess that I'm Quill," I answered; he seemed a little puzzled by that.

"My momma named us after her favorite things; I've got a brother named Whisky and two more sisters named Sugar and Honey," he said with a touch of pride in his voice.

"And the ferry is yours?"

"No. I just run it for Mister Perrin. He built it."

I nodded. "Mister Perrin pretty much runs Ferrypoint, doesn't he?"

"I guess so. You wouldn't notice unless you caused trouble, though. And folks who cause trouble don't stay long." He smiled, and it wasn't quite friendly. "It's a big river." I just nodded.

The next morning I started my duties as Perrin's apprentice. It was VERY hard work, with only a bit of instruction relative to the forge, but the conversation never slowed down for either work or instruction. We talked about ethics and metaphysics and ethics and political theory and more ethics. We drew an audience, when the main entrance to the forge was open. Pepper the vermite became a regular, sitting quietly with a brindled kitten in her lap.

I made the mistake of commenting on that; I asked Perrin if it struck him as odd that a vermite should have a pet cat, and Pepper smiled at me and said that it wasn't a pet, they raised cats for food. My jaw dropped open, and Perrin's hammer froze in mid-stroke. And then Pepper said, "Mister Perrin said I should tell you that, and it would be funny, but I don't get it." Perrin collapsed laughing, I considered dropping the anvil on him, and the kitten ran away; Pepper just stared at us as if we were insane.

The sun was setting on the seventh day of my apprenticeship as I closed the door to the forge and started putting away tools; Perrin was seated on a makeshift stool and filling his first pipe of the evening. The brindled kitten was playing suicidal tag with my feet, which she had been doing much of the time since Pepper's "food" joke. I didn't break my pace as I said, "Are you ever going to let me in, Perrin, or am I just another mark?"

Perrin looked up. "What's that, boy? I don't know what you're talking about."

I leaned on the anvil and looked at him. "As much as I've enjoyed the conversation, I know that conversation hasn't been your main goal. You've been selling me Elethay, and Valaria too, for that matter. I don't mind the activity, but I resent the subterfuge. I may not know who I am, but I do know that Elethay is at war with Jikadell, and that the Valarians carry Elethay's standard. I would wager a fair amount that you're an Elethay priest, at some level anyway, and that you're also a Valarian."

Perrin just looked at me calmly, but there was deep laughter from a back corner, and a well-dressed, handsome elf made his way through the clutter to join us. "He's calling your bluff, Perrin. I told you not to trifle with him," he said.

"Bluff nothing," Perrin told him. "I have to know who he is; it's my life on the line, and those who depend on me. But you have trouble remembering that, don't you?" The stranger just laughed.

"You would be Ravin," I said to the stranger, and something about him made me certain he had been the dragon in my dream-that-was-no-dream. "You didn't introduce yourself, last time."

Ravin smiled and extended his hand. "My apologies, Quill. But you didn't have a name to exchange, either, if you recall."

"No, I didn't. You seem awfully solid, for a ghost." I shook his hand, and all of my senses told me he was normal. Something else told me there was an aura of draconic power around him.

Ravin shrugged and smiled. "It's after sunset, and my ashes are in the river. Beyond that, I don't understand much more than you do, Quill. And Perrin-What do you want? I told you he used to be a necromancer; that explains the warp taint, he has done warp magic. And because of his magical training, he was able to bury the dragon inside himself. But he managed to actually kill off the necromancer inside of himself, somehow. I've never heard of such a thing before, but the proof is in front of you. And you KNOW that he attacked three warriors for the sake of a child who was a stranger. What do you want?"

Perrin looked at him, and then me, and then back at Ravin. Then he shrugged, then turned to me again. "All right then, boy... You said it yourself. There's a war on. Interested in signing up?"

I smiled. "That's it? You aren't going to tell me that if I really am a dragon, I have no hope of being neutral? That warp is EVIL, and that Jikadell and the necromancers are the real source of warp, and that shape shifters are just victims?"

Perrin scowled. "No point in telling you what you already know, boy."

"Perrin... There is an empty warehouse where my personality should be. I want a place to belong so badly it HURTS. And you offer me friendship, and then throw a cause in front of me that you are willing to DIE for. What do you think I am going to do?"

Ravin grinned; Perrin kept scowling and said, "Say it, boy. You need to say it."

23

I scowled back. "My life, my soul, and my honor for Elethay, for Valaria, and for Perrin Ironhand. Good enough?"

Ravin laughed behind his hand as Perrin's scowl collapsed into a broad smile; Perrin shook his head and said, "Good enough." Ravin looked at him, bowed elaborately to me, and vanished.

Three: Across the River

Half the grain and livestock produced in Kanchaka valley moves through the markets in Lechmore, and by livestock I mean human and elven slaves; that's what the market is for. You'd think there'd be a lot of money coming the other way, but you'd be wrong; the markets just exist to make it easier for the Haskalads to collect and distribute their feudal levies. Of course, drovers and bargemen and guards need to be paid, and nobles need to be entertained, and there is plenty of loose cash around for someone who knows how to look for it.

—Leod, the Storyteller of Freepost

Perrin went back to filling his pipe. "You know, I think this calls for a pub crawl," he said, once the pipe was drawing properly.

"Pub crawl?" I asked.

"It's time I introduced you to the only worthwhile thing about that rockpile across the river, boy," Perrin answered.

"And that would be?"

"The variety of tolerable beers. Also intolerable beers, but we try to avoid those..."

By the time full dark had arrived, Perrin and I were watching 'Bacco push the ferry out into the river; the windlass was locked, and 'Bacco assumed that it would be too much work for a vandal to haul the ferry in by chain. I watched the heavy links disappear into the river and agreed with him.

I wasn't ready for the nightlife in Lechmoor; every petty necromancer in the area (and there were many) seemed to be out showing off his most peculiar madspawn. And there were MANY very peculiar madspawn, only some of them fully controlled; I was very glad that Perrin had chosen to bring 'Bacco along.

Perrin started the tour at a place near the river that featured a fighting pit; a human who was built like 'Bacco and half again as tall was standing against all comers, ten Imps to try against 100 if you won. Perrin insisted that I pay close attention while three opponents were pummeled into unconsciousness, then led us away in search of better beer.

We were entering our fifth pub of the evening, a place called "The Severed Hand", which Perrin promised was going to be our last stop, when we were accosted by the warp elf I had dueled several days earlier. I had a quick thought about swimming home, but he was very polite and told us that his father wanted to meet me.

Father was easy to spot; like his son, he had batwings and ram's horns, but his clothes were much nicer, and his company was much more attractive: a winged female wakana and a winged female elf who had fine scales and an impressive spiked tail. The wakana was amazingly clean and well behaved (for a wakana), and the lizard girl was positively beautiful. Or rather she was beautiful until you looked into her eyes and saw the madness and bloodlust that comprised her entire personality.

The necromancer looked me over. "Do you like her? I am SO proud of her. She started as a beautiful Farillan girl, and each change has just made her more beautiful. I am Sojourner Braghia, by the way. I understand you have met my son Stragus."

"I am Quill," I answered, without extending my hand. "She is beautiful; it's a shame about her mind."

Sojourner shrugged; he seemed oblivious to my disapproval. "Not really. I don't keep her for conversation, after all." He laughed at that, as if it were terribly funny. Stragus and the wakana girl laughed; the lizard girl just looked around as if wondering whom she would be allowed to eat. "Well. You seem to have beaten some respect into my son's head. Are your services available?"

Perrin cut in. "He's my apprentice."

"Ah. Well. Perhaps you would be willing to loan him to me, for a time? It is not urgent; you may think about it. And you would be well paid." Perrin started to say something, but was stopped. "Away now," Sojourner flicked his hand at us, "The horse is on."

I looked at Perrin, who shrugged; we had been dismissed. We found a table as an ebony elf took the stage and checked the tuning on his harp; we managed to order our beer before the elf started to sing and silenced the room completely.

He was very, very good, both on the harp and as a singer. He was also physically striking, with the blue-black skin and silver-white hair of the Ebonese aristocracy. Perrin stared at the elf, muttered something under his breath, and shook his head. "Idiot," he said quietly; 'Bacco and I stared at him. "The fool's a shifter. And he has no defenses to speak of. He'll be lucky to live through the night."

The elf finished his song and nodded to the applause. The applause continued, and he stood and took a full bow; as he did so, a huge pair of feathered wings formed on his back; the crowd roared. "Yes, my friends," the elf said with a large smile, "I am Philo Majestic, the Pegasus Bard. And those of you in the audience who think that you could find better uses for my talents, please take the matter up with my master the Duke." There was a short silence as the significance of this sank in. "Unless you happen to be female, and promise that whatever you have in mind won't interfere with tomorrow's performance, in which case you can see me personally." There was general laughter, and then Philo seated himself and began another number.

Perrin continued to stare and mutter, "Idiot," occasionally; 'Bacco stared at Philo for a long time, then said, "He's lying. Bane doesn't know anything about him." Perrin looked at 'Bacco crossly; 'Bacco realized his mistake and cringed a bit, if you can imagine a boulder cringing.

I got up and did a slow drift toward the stage; I bought a drink for Philo and waited until he was between songs. I handed him the drink, and he looked at me quizzically. "When you need to run," I said, "and you will, cross the river and head for the forge. Try not to bring every necro in Lechmoor with you."

Philo's calm slipped for a split second. "Well," he said brightly, "that really isn't my style, but I'll keep it in mind." Then he scratched his nose and mouthed, "Thanks," from behind his hand.

After that we finally headed for home. Perrin's good mood had been ruined by Philo's stupidity, and once we were safely on the ferry and out of earshot of the shore he made no secret of it. "He'll end up on someone's warp altar, that's certain. I just hope he doesn't drag Bane up here in the process. We don't need him anywhere near this place."

"Maybe we can talk him into going underground, " I said.

Perrin scowled at me. "He's a peacock. He won't go underground, and it will kill him if he tries." He shrugged. "If he asks for help, we'll try. But I'm not hopeful."

"How did you know he was a shifter, before he announced it?" I asked.

"Valarian spell," 'Bacco offered; and Perrin scowled at him.

"Necros have a similar spell, and there's always someone in the crowd that is hoping to get lucky. I can dodge them, " Perrin explained. "'Bacco can't shift, and you're invisible for some reason. Philo stands out like a beacon, though." He shook his head sadly. "In the meantime... What did you think of Bosco?"

"The boxer? I think he'd make a great plow horse. Why?"

"Because I want you to take him on next week." My jaw dropped, and I saw
'Bacco's toothy grin out of the corner of my eye. "Don't say no just yet. Bosco won't be back on until the next big market day, so you'll have time to get ready."

I shook my head and said, "I'm beginning to think Philo may have the right idea," and 'Bacco guffawed; I decided to leave Perrin's admission that he was himself a shape-shifter for another time.

Several days later Perrin arrived at the forge wearing a smile that made me very nervous; it didn't help when he asked for the dagger on my belt. I wondered what new deviltry he had planned, but gave it to him; he gave me another dagger in return.

"This one is better steel, anyway," he said. "The claws are from that gilga you killed; one of the vermites back-tracked to it, and brought in the teeth and

29

claws. Thought you should have a souvenir. Or at least one you can see with your shirt on."

I examined the dagger carefully; it was a beautiful piece of work, obviously worth much more than the dagger I had given Perrin in exchange. The quillons were a pair of solidly set gilga claws, and there was a pair of gilga teeth set into the pommel. I looked up gratefully, and knew that I had been suckered, somehow.

"Now, about Bosco..." Perrin said, and I grimaced. "You can have the rest of the day to do whatever you want to get ready, but I want you back here and ready to cross the river at least an hour before sundown. You need to get over there, sign up, and get your bet down as early as you can, so that when I come hunting for you it will be believable."

I stared at him blankly. "My BET?"

Perrin shrugged. "MY bet then. I'm going to give you 350 to bet on yourself, and then as soon as the sun sets I am going to come over there screaming that you stole it and try to bully the tavern into giving the money back. They won't of course..."

I continued to stare blankly. "And the purpose of this is..."

"So that everyone knows that there is a lot of money on you, and that I think you're going to lose, soon enough that they can put bets down on Bosco."

I smiled and shook my head. "And where does this fit into being a Valarian Champion?"

It was Perrin's turn to stare blankly. "I'm a zealot, not a saint. There's a difference." Then he smiled. "Zealots have a lot more fun." I just shook my head and laughed.

Everything went according to plan; I crossed the river, signed up for my beating, and placed the bet. And then Perrin showed up and made a great deal of noise, which got him barred from the tavern until the fight started. And then he chased me up and down the waterfront and threatened to beat me to death with his cane, while I cringed and tried to apologize and 'Bacco held him back. I enjoyed it.

By the time I jumped into the pit with Bosco, the tavern was packed so tightly it was hard breathe. And then I got a fighter's eye view of Bosco, and began to dream of tying Perrin to the bottom of the ferry.

They called the start of the fight, and I hit Bosco so hard my hand hurt. He didn't seem to care. I ducked a punch that would have gone through a paneled wall, and hit him again. And again. And again. My fists were in agony, but Bosco was beginning to bleed, and he still hadn't managed to connect.

Seven punches. Eight. Bosco's face was a mess, but he didn't seem to mind, and I was getting tired; the crowd was beginning to complain that Bosco was throwing the fight. I wished them a great deal of ill.

Ten punches. Eleven. Twelve, and I was out of tricks; the hammer of the gods hit me squarely in the face, and I carommed off of the wall of the pit. I stumbled, and it saved me; Bosco was looking for me to still be at punching level, and seemed to be confused when I went down. I took a deep breath, got up as quickly as I could, and managed to land two more punches before the hammer fell again, this time on my right shoulder.

I spun around, my balance mostly lost, and managed to transfer my momentum into a side-of-the-left-hand backhand that caught Bosco in the corner of the jaw. He half turned with it, then turned back and looked me in the face as his knees gave out and he settled into the bottom of the pit.

I staggered back into a corner and leaned against the walls; several hands reached down to pull me up, but I didn't seem to be able to raise my arms. The crowd seemed to be happy, anyway. Someone jumped into the pit, and I recognized 'Bacco; he threw me over his shoulder, climbed out of the pit, and carried me out to the street.

Somehow we ended up at The Severed Hand. Perrin soon escorted his winnings home, and 'Bacco went with him; I found myself the recipient of a steady stream of congratulatory drinks, most of which I passed to Philo. Philo had commandeered the seat next to me as soon as he heard the news; he claimed to be writing a song about the fight, but spent most of the time between his performances absorbing large quantities of free alcohol.

Sojourner and his menagerie visited briefly; he had apparently made a fair bit of money on my fight, and expressed his gratitude. Stragus stayed with us, and managed to parlay a certain amount of reflected glory out of being my previous victim.

I took the liberty of asking Stragus why he was Warrior caste when his father was a Blazeblood noble; he just glared at me, but Philo answered. "His mother was a Farrilan slave; it limits his social possibilities."

Stragus glared at Philo. "At least my mother wasn't a damned horse."

Philo started to take offense at that, and then sighed. "No, she wasn't. And neither was my father; they were both perfectly normal, aside from being stupid enough to be taken as slaves." He looked at me hopelessly. "And I couldn't have been a dragon, or a unicorn, or even a werewolf. No, I get all of the disadvantages of being a shapeshifter in the most inoffensive package possible; I have to be a thrice damned birdy-horse." Stragus and I both pushed drinks in Philo's direction, and he downed them both in succession.

"There are plenty of stories of pegasus heroes," I ventured.

Philo snorted. "Messengers? Oh, and there was what's-his-name, who became famous by being the faithful steed and companion of a werewolf? No thank you." He found a glass that wasn't empty and drained it.

"The one I had in mind was the master swordsman of his era, but I don't suppose you would care about that," I answered.

Philo glared at me. "You're an orc. What do you know?"

"He can read," Stragus offered.

Philo looked from Stragus to me in confusion. "But... he's an ORC..." and something in his very soggy brain decided that that was enough for one night; his eyes glazed over and his face settled into the table.

I looked at Stragus, who owned the only face I recognized. "I think that marks the end of the party," I said. "Does anyone know where our friend here lives?"

"I'll take care of him," Stragus volunteered; I hesitated. The thought of turning a shapeshifter over to a warpspawn did not sit well with me. "My father is his real owner," Stragus whispered in my ear, "But Bane's name has more power. And the Duke hasn't been to Lechmoor in years."

I think I kept the surprise off of my face. "Have you seen 'Bacco?" I asked, "He was supposed to come back for me."

Stragus shook his head. "I sent him home. Come with me; my father has a special thank-you waiting for you."

I clenched my teeth and looked around the room. I didn't like the sound of that at all, but I was alone in a city of necromancers and warpspawn. "Really?" I answered. "How very nice of him."

Four: A Night With Jikadell

See those two women glaring at each other, the one in the green, and the one in the blue? There's enough hatred there to heat a barn through a blizzard. You usually don't see both temples out in the open like this; if necromancers are in charge, worshipping Elethay will get you killed, and if Elethay is in charge, worshipping Jikadell will get you killed. Of course, when you realize that most of Jikadell's yellow girls are really just whorehouse slaves, it doesn't come as much of a surprise that most of them pray to Elethay every night for rescue. And both of those women know it, and both of them go to sleep every night thinking about it. The difference is that the one in blue laughs, and the one in green cries.

—Leod, the Storyteller of Freepost

Stragus summoned his servants from wherever they had been hiding, and the group carried Philo away. To me, Stragus would only say that I was to go to the temple, introduce myself, and say that I was a guest of Baron Braghia. He seemed envious of me; I was beginning to be envious of Philo.

I was tired, and sore, and feeling VERY alone; the idea of spending a night in the Warp Queen's whorehouse did not appeal to me at all. On the other hand, refusing was likely to offend Sojourner, and that was not something I wanted to deal with either. With luck, I would be able to plead my injuries, find a place to sleep, and bypass most of the problems.

When Elethay is presented in three phases, they are the Red Warrior, the Green Mother, and the Gray Sage. Jikadell's counterparts to these are the Yellow Harlot, the Blue Dominatrix, and the Black Sorceress. Not much contest, to my mind, but Jikadell offers the incentive of Warp Magic, and that makes the difference, sometimes. It did for the Haskalads, anyway. And this was a Haskalad city, and I was standing on the threshold of a Haskalad Temple.

The male door wardens passed me without comment; once inside, I introduced myself to a scantily clad female who cringed at every word I spoke. She led me into the temple, and moments later I was standing before a scaled and winged woman who might have been the sister of Sojourner's pet, except that this one had intelligence to match the malice in her eyes. I didn't think we were likely to be friends.

"You?" she hissed. "You're Braghia's new protégé? How... sad." We stared at each other for some moments. "I suppose I should introduce myself, but I really can't be bothered." She glared at one of her attendants. "Take him to the West Suite, and keep him out of my sight as he leaves." The indicated girl beckoned to me urgently; I shrugged and followed.

The first thing I saw when I entered the West Suite was the girl, and my eyes rebelled, so I took in the rest of the room. It was dominated by a large bed that looked comfortable, if you neglected the manacles; the walls were decorated with a wide assortment of minor torture devices. I closed my eyes and clenched my teeth.

I heard the door close behind me and steeled myself to look at the girl. She was a Farrilan elf, dressed in a minimal combination of sheer silks and brooches. She was sitting on her heels, and her hands clasped her ankles; her head was bowed, and she was trembling slightly. She said, "How my I serve my master?" without looking up.

I shook my head and bit back a laugh; this was not a situation I had expected. I knelt in front of the girl, lifted her chin to reveal an ethereally beautiful face, and said softly, "You can start by not being afraid, and by telling me your name."

"You're an orc! I thought you were going to be a warpspawn!" She seemed genuinely surprised, but then she realized what she had done. "I mean... My name is Chalice Autumnleaf, master."

I shook my head. "Quill, Chalice, not 'Master'. And all I want is a good night's sleep; I've been battered too much to care about anything else. So PLEASE stop being afraid."

She looked into my face. "Battered? By the Lady! Both of your eyes have been blackened! What happened?" She seemed genuinely concerned, and it distracted her from her fear.

"I won a fight I knew better than getting into. I'll heal."

"I can help," she said. "I can make a poultice, and there are spells..."

"No magic." I didn't quite bark it; Chalice recoiled as if I had hit her. "I have to accept the bed by the rules of hospitality, but I want nothing of Jikadell's magic. Understood?" I pulled off my boots and shirt, got into bed, and tried to sleep.

Chalice left the room briefly, and returned with some sort of paste that she applied to my face, and then she tied a bandage full of the stuff to my shoulder. She talked softly to herself as she worked; I didn't pay much attention. Then suddenly I felt SOMETHING...

I sat up with a lurch and clamped her wrist in my hand. "I said NO MAGIC." I forced her to her knees with pressure and torsion; her face contorted with pain.

"Witchcraft," she gasped, as tears started to flow. "Elethay's magic."

"You're a witch?" I let her go. "In a Jikadell temple?" She nodded; she was beginning to sob. I put my hands on her shoulders and pulled her into my arms. "I am sorry I hurt you. What happened? How did a witch end up as a Jikadell whore?" Her only answer was to bury her head against my chest and continue sobbing. I let her cry herself out; there didn't seem to be much other choice. Eventually she got control of herself and told me her story.

She had been an acolyte in an Elethay temple in a place called Arecha, which my mental maps told me was several hundred miles to the west. She had had a vision about the fate of a famous artifact, and had followed it to the Celestial Kingdom, and then into the Haskalad Empire, where she had been enslaved and made to serve Jikadell. She had changed hands several times before arriving in Lechmoor, and now her quest had come to a very different end than she had envisioned.

"Always before, I had been planning to escape, but now... they need me. Most of the other... women... here are Elethay worshipers at heart, and they look to me for healing, and for guidance. Clytemnestra thinks we are all disposable, and only cares about the Haskalads that are working as acolytes of the Yellow Harlot until they can become priestesses of the Blue Dominatrix. So even if I knew where to go next, I don't think I could leave without a clear sign from the Lady that it was her will..."

I held her tightly against my side and stroked her hair with my free hand. "And what is it that you have been chasing, Chalice? What is this precious artifact? And where do you think it is?"

"It's an Alicorn. Or it was... One of my ancestors was a unicorn, and died in that form... With his own consent, his horn was made into a dagger;

it is tied to Scavian the Boatman, somehow."

"I begin to see why you have been chasing it." I paused for a moment, and summoned what I knew of the legends of the Boatman. "How is it tied to Scavian?"

"It can be used to summon him, sometimes even to places he would not normally go. I'm not sure how it works, I just know where it is. Or at least I have an idea."

"And what would that idea be?" I asked. "I have a great number of maps in my head, maybe I can help you." Chalice looked into my eyes, wondering if she could trust me. "I swear to you by the Lady we both serve that, if I should ever have this dagger in my hands, I will see that it is returned to you, or to your people in Arecha. Good enough?"

She smiled. "Good enough." She pulled herself closer to me, and talked into my shoulder. "The last person to have the alicorn dagger was a distant aunt of mine, the sister of my great, great grandmother, who was also named Chalice. In my dream, she is high on the side of a mountain; ahead of her is the mountain peak, and it looks... evil, somehow. And behind her there is a ridge of mountains, and at the far end there is a single mountain that seems to be glowing white.

"And then there is a rockslide," she continued. "Chalice is buried beneath it, and the Alicorn with her. She dies there. But then, over the years, a large tree grows up, and its roots find Chalice's body, and wrap themselves around her. And then there is a great storm, and the tree is uprooted, and Chalice's remains, and the alicorn dagger, are pulled back to the surface. And the very last thing in the dream is a view of Chalice's skeleton, and what remains of her clothing, and I can see the brooch she was using to hold her cloak closed. It is a vertical oval, with a black stone at the top, and a white stone in the center, with line or a connection between the two."

I thought about that, and my mind went back to Jasmine drawing in the flour on the countertop, and the things I had learned about Kanchaka geography since then. "Do you have any idea what it means, Chalice?"

"Not really." She rolled onto her back and stared at the ceiling; her face was very sad in the dim light. "I went to the Celestial Kingdom to look at maps, but never found any that helped. And I have seen brooches like that; I even bought one. I found out that they came from the Kanchaka valley, but no one could explain what they meant. So I tried to come here, and, well, I guess I succeeded. But not very well. And I still don't know where the dagger is."

I chuckled. "Then again…" I propped my head on my left hand, and reached across Chalice's body with my right. I touched her side above her left hip with my right finger. "This is the pass into the Haskalad Empire." I ran my finger up to her ribs, then around the base of her ribcage, down to her right hip, and and back across to the left. "Mountains." I indicated her navel. "A pristine mountain called Goldentooth." I ran my finger up the shallow furrow to the base of her breastbone. "Blighted ridge. And here…" I tapped the base of her breastbone. "Is a highly warped mountain called Blackwater. And I am willing to bet there is an uprooted tree somewhere on its south face."

Chalice propped herself on her elbows and stared at the invisible map I had drawn. "And where are we?" she asked; her voice trembled.

I indicated a point just below her ribs and left of the center. "About here. Less than a hundred miles, I think."

Chalice continued to stare, and started to shake her head. "So close. But… Quill, what should I do? What CAN I do?"

"Can you stand to stay here a while longer?" I asked; she nodded. "Then let me get it, and bring it to you. And in the meantime perhaps the Lady will tell you if she wants you to stay here." There was a long silence as she continued to stare at her abdomen, then she pounced on me and hugged me fiercely enough to make my injured shoulder twinge.

After a moment, I said, "Can I please get some sleep now?" Chalice pulled away and looked at me with curiousity; I could only shake my head. "This is a temple to Jikadell. I do not want to do ANYTHING that could be taken as an act of worship to her. You should understand that." Chalice nodded and started to get up; I took her hand. "But you're welcome to share the bed, if you would like. I am only concerned about what the goddesses know; I don't care about appearances." Chalice smiled at that, and relaxed. I kissed her hand, and fell asleep.

Sometime later I found myself awake, watching Chalice sleep with an uncomfortable combination of affection and raw lust. I saw a human male materialize out of the stone wall and quietly scoop up most of the contents of the food platter Chalice and I hadn't touched. I realized that he had his eye on the pile of my belongings, and I clicked my tongue. He was startled for a moment, then looked right at me and smiled. He bowed, made a rude gesture, and dissolved back into the wall.

In the morning, I asked Chalice about our visitor while I was dressing to leave. She was aware of him, but didn't know much more about him than I did.

"We call him the Hungry Ghost, or just Ghost," she said. "No one knows where he comes from, though we think it must be somewhere inside the temple grounds. Sometimes he even talks to some of the girls, but only to ask them questions. "

I arrived at the ferry pier in the false dawn, and watched 'Bacco arrive at the pier across the river and prepare the ferry for its first crossing, then cross to me. I jumped on before the ferry touched the pier, and 'Bacco switched directions to take me home. I leaned heavily against the south rail of the ferry as I watched him. We were in the middle of the river when the sun's first rays hit us, and they turned the entire river to gold. I felt the sun on my face, and closed my eyes.

"Long night?" 'Bacco asked.

"Tobacco, my friend," I answered, "The Lady Elethay is occasionally cruel, and can have a wicked sense of humor." He didn't answer that, and I continued. "I spent the night in the arms of a beautiful woman, in a brothel no less, and the result is that I am frustrated beyond imagining. And for the sake of the Lady, and my own conscience, I can't even WISH that things were any different." I shook my head and shrugged.

'Bacco laughed, and then I laughed, and then 'Bacco snorted, and eventually 'Bacco was stretched full length on the deck of the ferry, pounding the planks with his fists, while I attempted to operate the windlass. 'Bacco's blows echoed across the river in the morning quiet. His hat fell off, and I used it to drench him in river water, which calmed him down a bit. He left me to turn the windlass until we were close enough for me to jump, though. He was still giggling as he pulled back across the river to take up his morning's station on the east shore.

I had opened the smithy and stoked the forge before I noticed the bundle on the floor; there was a note attached to it that read, "A smart gambler always tips the winner. —Perrin." I opened the bundle to find a greatsword that was fitted with gilga claws to match the dagger Perrin had given me earlier. I unwrapped it carefully and swung it through a few flourishes; it was as beautiful to handle as it was to look at.

I turned to see Perrin leaning against the doorway smiling at me. "You earned it, boy," he said, and there was a note of genuine affection in his voice. "Now put it away and get back here; you've still got yesterday's work to do."

Five: Into the Woods

You come down with the Tox, and if you're lucky, you recover. If you're less lucky, you die. If your luck is bad, you change, and maybe you go mad. How do you change? Hard to say. You might grow wings, or horns, or breath fire, or all of them. You might turn into a plant, or a genius, or an idiot. But you WILL be left with a craving for Warp, and a hunger for another mutation, and another... Pretty soon there won't be any YOU left, and if you meet your best friend, you might kill him for food, or just to see the interesting colors as you tear him apart. But you WILL kill him; that's what madspawn do.

—Leod, the Storyteller of Freepost

I stowed the sword in my cellar room and received a scolding for my truancy from Brindle the kitten, who had decided to adopt me. I tangled her up in the blanket, which she seemed to take as an apology, because she followed me up to the forge.

I told Perrin everything I had learned the night before; about Philo and his relationship to Sojourner, about Chalice and her dagger, and about my strange meeting with the Hungry Ghost. Perrin made no comment except those relevant to the forge. When I had finished, he just stood and looked at me for a while.

"And what are you going to do about that promise, boy?" he asked; I couldn't tell if he approved or not.

"Get your advice, of course. What else?"

He laughed at that. "Did you manage to hold onto your winnings?" When I nodded, he continued, "Then see Jasmine about getting some leathers made up; you're going to need them. I'll talk to Whisky about the details." I nodded again, and then we went on about the day's business.

Ten days went by. I knew Perrin well enough that I didn't remind him of my promise to Chalice, but the wait was beginning to wear on me; I felt as if every conversation was based on NOT discussing Chalice and her dagger. A beautiful suit of hunter's leathers was hanging in my room (much to Brindle's amusement), but the topic never came up. And then one afternoon Whisky walked into the smithy.

I hadn't met Whisky before. If 'Bacco looked like a cross between a rat and a plowhorse, Whisky looked like a cross between a rat and a pine tree. He wasn't just tall for a vermite, he was tall in any company, and so thin that one assumed his leathers were holding his bones together. He looked at me for a moment, spat a stream of something noxious at my feet, and turned to Perrin.

"He's going to die, you know that," he said. "We ought to strip him naked first, for all the good his hardware will do him. Then it won't be a total loss."

Perrin just shrugged and turned to me. "Have you met Whisky, Quill? He's probably the most cheerful person you'll ever meet."

I said, "No, I haven't," and offered Whisky my hand; he stared at me a while, and then shook my hand about a heartbeat before I decided to withdraw it. He showed me just enough teeth to let me know that it was a trick that he practiced and was proud of.

"It's like this," Whisky said, sketching a circle on the dirt floor with his spear. "First you climb the base of the mountain, which takes you up above the clouds, where the air would be hard to breathe even if there was no warp burn. It's not a hard climb, but the warp burn is the worst I've ever seen; you don't need any magical training at all to feel it eating at you. There's no fallen tree like your whore described anywhere there, and you can't see Goldentooth from the top, anyway."

He sketched another circle, just inside the first one. "So once you get up to here, you've got yourself a moor. Swamps and sinkholes and standing stones and fog that never, ever goes away. And anything that you see that's alive is so Tox-twisted it wishes it wasn't. And in the middle of THAT…" He drew a third circle, about half the diameter of the second one. "Here you have another mountain. Don't know much about it; I've never been stupid enough to try to cross the moor. Figure that's where your tree is, though. I was high up on the north side of Goldentooth, once, and I could see Blackwater's Fang, so I imagine you can see Goldentooth from the side of the Fang, too."

"So how are we going to get there?" I asked; I was too excited to actually LISTEN to what Whisky was saying.

"WE are not going to get there at all. I am going to get you onto the moor, and then YOU are going to wander around until you get yourself killed, and then I am going to come home." He grinned at me.

Perrin shook his head. "Just bring back the dagger, boy. And try to be careful."

We left with the dawn the next morning. Whisky was a better companion than I expected, and he seemed to have memorized every rock and tree we passed. I asked him how long he had been hunting in these woods.

"Ten, twelve years, maybe more," he said. "Depending on how you count, as to when I stopped being a noisy kid that tagged along and started to pull my own weight. My Uncle Barley would probably tell you that happened later than I would." He grinned again. "I KNOW I was worth the trouble before I was full grown, probably by the time I was eight or so."

I looked at him; in human terms, I would have thought him a well-weathered 40. "How old are you? If I may ask?"

Whisky shrugged. "Nineteen. Two years older than 'Bacco, ten years older than Pepper. I don't think you've met my other two sisters."

That startled me a bit; I searched my memory for knowledge of vermites, and found little; the rat folk were just part of the background, which I think is the way they liked it. "Pepper is NINE?"

"Nearly ten. Why, what'd you think?"

"As an elf, I'd say mid-twenties; human, 15 or 16. But... NINE?"

Whisky shrugged again. "Momma was only 11 when I was born; there's plenty of bucks around wish Pepper would get in the game and have pups of her own. She's in no hurry, and no one-no rat folk, anyway-is going to push. Not when she's 'Bacco's sister, and not now that she's your friend. We tend to hide from trouble," he said, and gave me another of those smug grins. "Our mommas teach us to avoid the stomping foot, and if you can't avoid it, make sure you bite it good and hard."

I shook my head and laughed at that; there didn't seem to be much else to say.

Whisky kept us walking until nearly sundown, when he led me into a nicely sheltered hollow with a cache of firewood already gathered. I commented on this, and Whisky just shrugged; he said that it never hurt to have something stowed away for a bad time.

"It's no fun to search for firewood when you're bleeding, and there's a dragon storm on your heels. And it's not much trouble to stock a decent spot by daylight, particularly when you've got fresh meat and nowhere to go." Whisky looked at me, as if waiting for me to pass judgement; I didn't. "I put more into the clan than I take out, and then some. I don't mind someone else getting fat on my work, as long as I get to get fat, too."

Whisky soon had a fire going, and a pot of stew bubbling away. I laid out my bedroll and watched Whisky work while I thought about the day's events, and the day's conversation.

"Whisky, why would it matter to the other vermites that Pepper is my friend? They don't think I have a claim on her, do they?"

Whisky snorted at that. "Not if you don't want it. But it's not an issue; we don't keep much track of fathers, pups just belong to the clan. I think Uncle Barley sired me, but it doesn't matter." He stopped to stir the stew. "But you... What happened to the last fellow who didn't listen when Pepper said, 'No'?"

"So they're afraid of me?"

"No, they're afraid of Pepper." He chuckled at that. "You, it's more like awe."

"What about you?"

Whisky snorted. "I don't do awe much. You're a good fighter, and you seem to be a decent person. It's a shame you're going to be dead so soon."

My eyes widened. "You're that sure?"

He shrugged. "I know what I know. Perrin, he talks to the dead, and he talks to the Lady herself, sometimes, so when he says to take you out and let you lose yourself on Blackwater, I do it. But that doesn't make it make any more SENSE." He shook his head. "Grab a bowl of this before the company gets here."

The stew was excellent; I had just taken a second helping when Whisky's "company" arrived; an enormous yellow she-wolf and an even bigger black male. Whisky gave them each a bowl of stew, which they ate greedily. Whisky introduced them as "Light" and "Shadow", and I couldn't help but feel that the female rolled her eyes at the introduction.

"These two are the reason this stretch of woods is so pleasant," Whisky said. "Five years ago, there were drakkels all over. Then Lady Light showed up, and a while after that Shadow, and they went to war. And now there are no drakkels at all, and the hunting is almost TOO easy." He flipped a piece of jerky at Shadow's ear, and the huge head snapped around to catch it with terrifying speed. "Shadow is a fiend for salt. Lady Light is MUCH more polite." He waved a piece of jerky at Light, and she came forward to take it from his hand.

When supper was done Whisky banked the fire and we bedded down. Shadow took a position outboard of Whisky, and Light was outboard of me. I rolled that way and looked at the firelight reflected in her eyes. "You could talk if you wanted to," I said quietly; Light just cocked her head to one side. I shook my head and said, "Amazing." Light slowly rolled her head back upright, and then gave me one short nod.

The wolves stayed with us the next day, and by sunset we had reached another of Whisky's caches. This one was at the base of the south face of Blackwater, and it towered over us. "This is where you want to come, if you do manage to ever get off of the moor," Whisky told me. "Even if I'm not here, there's water, and firewood, and I'll show you where I hide emergency rations. And then wait; Perrin will know if you're still alive, and as long as you are, I'll come and look for you every week or so. So just wait."

The following day we climbed up to the moor itself; the wolves left us as soon as they saw where we were going. About mid-day we crossed a small pass, and could see the moor spread out a few feet below us; as promised, it was covered in thick fog.

"I've had about as much warp burn as I want already; time to part company," Whisky said. "Try to remember everything, every last rock and crevice. Go slow, and be careful."

I nodded. "Care to give me odds?"

Whisky looked at me. "Sure. Ten to one against you. Easy."

I fished a coin out of a pocket and handed it to him. "I see you again, you owe me ten."

He looked at the coin and grinned. "Done. But hauntings don't count."

I nodded. "Hauntings don't count." And I headed down onto the moor.

By the time I made my first night's camp I was hopelessly lost, and wondering what had possessed Perrin to send me on this fool's errand. I had plenty of supplies, and could live on the foul water and stunted vegetation that lived on the moor, if I had to, but the warp burn would kill me in a fortnight.

The land seems to like orcs, for some reason, even horribly warped land like Blackwater Moor. I did my best to listen to whatever was orcish within me, and tried to stretch my supplies by foraging; I was awakened more than once by various small ambushers, but they always ducked out of the way before I could add them to my menu. My journal for that period is almost amusing; it consists of the word "lost" as an entire entry for eight consecutive days.

On the ninth day I met a pair of rats, each of which outweighed me. They thought that I looked like an easy meal; I tried to convince them otherwise. I tried to keep them far enough apart that I would only have to deal with one at a time, but it was miserable, nerve wracking work; I could outmaneuver them easily, but I could not hope to match their four-legged gallop when it came to covering ground. Still, I managed to hit each of them three times and only took one bite in return; I was beginning to feel I might survive the encounter when I fell into a hole.

I almost quit. If my sword hadn't been tethered to my right wrist, I probably would have just lain there. But I could hear the rats experiment with ways to follow me into the hole, and I knew where my weapon was; I staggered to my feet.

Killing the rats was amazingly easy; they were unable to defend themselves as they climbed down, and I didn't give them the chance to finish the climb. That done, I looked up at the miserable gray mess that passed for sky on Blackwater Moor and offered my soul to Elethay. I could climb out, with some effort, but there didn't seem to be much point; between the rat bite and the fall, I was only a day away from death by warp burn.

As my eyes grew accustomed to the darkness, I found a shelf on the side of my pit that led to a fairly dry alcove; I climbed into it and made what was certain to be my last camp. I did my best to dry out my clothing, which had become drenched in the course of my flight from the rats; by sunset I was warm, fairly dry, and as comfortable as my warp-ravaged body would allow.

I wrapped myself in my blanket, and prepared to die.

Six: Dealing with the Dead

Valeria has been dead for 300 years now, and she lived for more than two centuries. She spent most of that time trying to warn the dragons that doom was coming, and they ignored her, and let it come. Their spirits were off on the Spirit Plane, participating in a huge Day of the Dead ceremony, and the necromancers broke in and sucked out their souls. Four out of five dragons in the world died in that raid, and so much Warp was let loose into the world that the storms didn't calm down for fifty years. The only good thing was that the necromancers immediately turned on each other, trying to decide who was going to be boss. They're still at it, which is the main reason I wasn't strangled for my big mouth years ago.

—Leod, the Storyteller of Freepost

I found that I was riding in a boat of some kind on a vast and eerily calm sea that extended to the horizon in three directions. I was drifting slowly toward a nearly featureless shore. A wolf that was the color of old mahogany paced the shore as if waiting for me to arrive.

Later, the wolf became a woman in brilliant crimson armor, though I do not remember the change; she reached out and stopped my boat before it touched the shore. Her hair matched the color of the wolf's fur.

"Are you in such a hurry to walk the sunless lands, Little Brother?" the woman asked. I tried to answer, but could not; I tried to shake my head and failed. "I don't think you are. But such is not your fate, anyway; you have a few more miles to travel, I think." She smiled warmly as she spoke, then pushed the boat back out into deeper water. "And when you meet my old friend Stormchaser, Little Brother, tell her that Valaria says it is time for her to come home."

Valaria? I woke up with a start, and realized that I was still at the bottom of a hole on Blackwater Moor. I felt much better for resting, though, and judged from the brightness of the gloom (an odd phrase, but appropriate for the bottom of a hole) that it must be about mid-day. I looked at the festering bodies of the rats I had killed the previous day, and the sight made me hungry; I tried not to think about what I was doing as I drew my dagger and carved a generous portion of raw rancid rat.

I spent ten days in that hole, broken only by ever lengthening forays onto the moor; I had become well enough acquainted with the substance of the moor that I was able to take Whisky's advice and memorize every rock. I consumed both of the rats that had followed me into the pit, as well as a third that had hoped to improve upon its fellow's fortunes; I passed time by using rodent shoulder blades to practice my scrimshaw. I spent the twentieth night since leaving Whisky camped on the moor, but retreated to my friendly hole for the twenty-first. I spent another day there recovering from warp burn, and then, on the twenty-third day of my explorations, I found the Fang, and within a few hours, Chalice's overturned tree.

I climbed out into the sunlight, circled to the high side of the tree, and eventually saw a mummified body high in the huge mass of severed roots. I climbed carefully to the body, saw the dagger, reached out to take it...

A bolt of crimson energy knocked me loose from the tree and I tumbled to the ground; I started to rise and a second bolt knocked me flat again. I decided to try negotiation.

"Chalice!" I called. "Chalice Stormchaser! Your kinswoman— Your niece— Chalice Autumnleaf sent me. I have come to bring the Alicorn back to your people." I heard hooves on the scree, and soon there was a unicorn standing over me, threatening to finish me off with its horn. It was vaguely translucent in the harsh sunlight. I waited, and the unicorn metamorphosed into an elven woman who, save for the translucency, looked like a more robust version of the living Chalice.

"My kin sent you?" the ghost asked.

I risked rising to my elbows. "Yes," I answered. "And you have my word, before Elethay, that I will do all that I can to restore the Alicorn to your Kin. May I rise?"

The ghost offered me her hand and helped me to my feet; I looked at the tree and then into her eyes; she had been alone with the warp creatures since the Death Day massacre was only a little regarded prophecy. There were three hundred years of loneliness in that handshake, and in those eyes. "Do you swear it?" she said, and there was hunger in her voice.

"On my soul," I answered, and she threw her arms around me and wept ghostly tears. "I have a message, also," I said. "A woman with dark red hair said to me, 'And when you meet my old friend Stormchaser, Little Brother, tell her that Valaria says it is time for her to come home.' Be free, Chalice." The ghost kissed my cheek, and disappeared.

The climb was more difficult the second time, but I managed it. The dagger and its sheath were still in excellent condition, but the same could not be said of Stormchaser's earthly remains. I felt a bit of remorse at leaving the body there, but had little choice; I was too badly injured for heavy labor. Beyond that, I knew that her spirit was free, finally. I took the brooch that the living Chalice had seen in her dream, and gathered the buttons and buckles

53

on the assumption that Chalice, or her family, might want keepsakes.

I found a secure seat and looked to the south, across the grey soup of the moor, down Blighted Ridge to Goldentooth in the distance. It was peaceful, and melancholy; I could easily have slept there. And then something inside me with weaker aesthetic sensibilities and a great deal more sense reminded me that I was breathing thin and warp tainted air, and that if I didn't get moving my friends were going to give me up for dead. I laughed out loud at that thought, and very carefully made my way back to the moor, and my homey little sump.

I spent another eight days in that hole recovering from Stormchaser's efforts at protecting her legacy. Two more rats donated their bodies to my disgusting larder while I waited to heal; my scrimshaw gradually improved.

The dagger that had caused me so much trouble was a beautiful thing, at any rate; it was as long as my forearm, impossibly sharp, and looked to have been carved from a single piece of opal. I wondered at the magic that had gone into its creation, and wondered again at what it might be capable of in the right hands.

Eventually I began the final leg of my adventure on Blackwater moor, which was finding a path from my hole to the outer rim, and then back to Ferrypoint. It was slow and miserable work, moving in ever widening circles, always making sure that I was within sight of terrain I had memorized, always waiting for another rat-or something worse-to ambush me. I decided that I could risk two full days of exploration before returning to the hole to recuperate-but that meant another two days in the hole before I ventured out again.

One afternoon I came upon the carcass of a dead and badly decayed gilga spawn, and was hungry enough to carve off a piece; the gilga protested. There was no question that it was long dead, but apparently the local warp had managed to animate its decaying body. I backed carefully toward shelter, and was horrified to learn that, rotten as it was, it was still able to fly.

I was much better armed and armored than the last time I had faced a gilga, but death had given this thing a durability that stretched belief. I hit it again and again, and had little difficulty evading its claws, but eventually I was too tired to dodge and it was still moving. We traded blows twice, to my extreme detriment, and then I finally managed to sever its head, and it stopped fighting. I chopped it into small pieces, and ate several of them, even though they were disgusting even by my horrible recent standards. And then I retreated back to my hole.

Fifty-one days after parting company with Whisky I found my way back to the camp he had shown me; I had been missing from Ferrypoint almost twice as long as I had lived there. I wondered how long I should wait for Whisky before I tried to find my way on my own, but Whisky and the wolves arrived three days after I did.

The wolves were extremely cautious of me at first, and Whisky just stared in horror; I shrugged. "I figure I'm going to disappear into the river for about an hour when we get back, and I'm probably going to have to burn the clothes," I said.

Whisky nodded. "You can say that twice. How much of that garbage is your own blood?"

"Enough." I indicated the tears in my leathers, and the wounds underneath. "This is from a rat that outweighed me, and these two are from a gilga that had already been dead for a couple of weeks, at least." Whisky just gaped at that, and I shrugged. "It's a strange place. Have you ever had a unicorn do that 'red death' thing to you? I have, twice. AND taken two really bad falls. And then there was the warp burn…"

"And the reason you're still alive is…"

I shrugged again. "I got lucky. I fell into a hole and found a refuge from the warp."

I handed him one of the gilga's shoulder blades. "That's a pretty good map, from the rim to the hole I stayed in, to the base of the Fang. Just in case anybody ever wants to go back. In the meantime… You DID bring the stew pot, didn't you? I'm about ready to kill for some hot food."

Whisky laughed at that, and soon had a meal prepared. After we had eaten, he looked at me again and asked, "Was it worth it?"

"I don't know," I answered, and showed him the dagger. "I am inclined to think so."

"Warp and insanity, that's beautiful! It's a shame to see it locked up in a Jikadell temple, of all places."

I shook my head. "It's up to Chalice. I hope she decides to leave the temple; I know she wants to; she hates it there. But she feels the other women need her." Whisky just shook his head.

The two-day walk to Ferrypoint was uneventful; my homecoming was delightfully anticlimactic. Perrin groused about all of the work I had missed, and grinned when he thought I wasn't looking; Jasmine hugged me, then scolded me for the hideous damage I had done to her leatherwork; 'Bacco grinned and said he would spot me to a drink at the 'Hand as soon as I had gotten cleaned up. Brindle the kitten (who had doubled in size while I was gone) bit me once as hard as she could, and then treated me as if I had never left.

The Alicorn impressed the gallery, though. Jasmine said that the sheath was unicorn leather impregnated with Moonglow odylic; Perrin marveled at the dagger's flexibility and sharpness. We spent some time in speculation on what would cause a unicorn to want his corpse to be treated in such a fashion, and then I went off to try to wash Blackwater out of my hair.

A long bath and a change of clothes later, 'Bacco and I were sitting in the Severed Hand, listening to Philo charm another audience. When he had finished his set, he joined us, and seemed genuinely glad to see me.

"I heard you were having an adventure," Philo gushed. "I hope you have a couple of good stories to tell."

I resisted an urge to show him the Alicorn; I suspected that it might cause a riot. "I might. But at the moment, I need your help. I need to talk to the Jikadell girl that Sojourner set me up with the night I fought Bosco. How do I go about that?"

Philo stared at me as if I were the stupidest creature on the planet. "You pay your money and you pick her out of the line. Or you pay more money and you make a reservation. Or you pay even more money, and they throw out whoever she's with, and bring her to you…"

I smiled half-heartedly. "I only want to TALK, Philo…"

Philo sighed. "So you pay your money, and you pick her out of the line, or…" I started to growl, and he stopped. "They're slaves, Quill. And as far as Clytemnestra cares, they only exist for the revenue. Tell her you want to butcher one alive, and she'll quote you a price. So it doesn't matter WHAT you want, it will cost you money."

I nodded. "You sound like the voice of experience."

Philo grinned. "No, I've been listening to Stragus. He's become obsessed with one of them, and she doesn't like him, so he beats her. Which makes her less valuable to the temple, which makes the rate they charge him go UP. Which makes him that much angrier, and he beats her that much more… I figure the poor girl has about a week before he kills her."

"You sound like you find it amusing," I said, flat voiced.

Philo looked at me, and for a moment his desperation flashed across his face, then he shook it off. "It comes of having a price one's head. It tends to… broaden… one's perspective." 'Bacco growled, and I just shook my head.

We left the 'Hand as soon as Philo began his next set and made our way to the temple. We were told that Chalice was engaged, but that she would be free at midnight, and that her services for the second half of the night would cost 20 Imperials. 'Bacco and I had 26 between us; I sent 'Bacco home with six, and sat down to wait.

Philo's lecture on the nature of Jikadell the Harlot's trade BOTHERED me. I found myself resisting an urge to strangle everyone I saw who wasn't wearing the yellow silk of the temple whores. I wanted to call fire from the sky and blast the temple, and Lechmoor, and the whole Haskalad Empire right off the face of the earth. All I did was sit quietly and wait for my turn.

It was a long wait; they tried to talk me into visiting another girl. Eventually they brought me to Chalice's room; I was reminded that I had not paid for the privilege of damaging her, and would be well advised to refrain from doing so. I kept my comments to myself.

The room was much smaller than the one I had first visited, and empty save for the bed and the girl; Chalice knelt in the same position as the last time. I sat down in front of her cross-legged before she could choke out the standard greeting. She looked up in surprise; she said, "Quill?" and her voice broke.

All of my anger slid back to somewhere outside of that room, and I smiled at her with all of the warmth I had. "Did you think I had forgotten?" Chalice threw her arms around me, hugged me fiercely, and shook her head against my shoulder. I chuckled and hugged back.

"It's been awful, Quill. I think they may kill me soon, just for amusement." She paused, and fought back the sobs that were trying to make themselves heard. "I don't mind dying, Quill. Especially not in the Lady's service. But I want so much to know that I am doing what she wants."

I pushed her away and kissed her forehead. "This may help," I said, and pulled the Alicorn from my belt pouch. She stared as I unwrapped it; I got the impression she was afraid to touch it. I took it out of its sheath and presented the hilt to her; she took it tentatively and then doubled up in pain and dropped it.

I grabbed the Alicorn reflexively, started to reach for Chalice, and then stopped and got out of the way while a miracle took place. Chalice's mass multiplied; her bones lengthened and shifted, and in the space of a few heartbeats she had become a unicorn. She made a loud and frightened equine noise, and I gestured her to silence. I threw a blanket across her shoulders, and then wrapped my arms around her neck. "Slowly, Chalice. Just relax and be quiet."

Chalice's breathing slowed to a normal rate, and I said, "Now… Do you have any idea how to change back?" She started to shake her head, then stopped to look at me and nodded once. And then she was herself again. I picked her up and sat on the bed; she held onto me with all of her strength and trembled.

"I think," I said quietly, "That we can take that as a sign that the Lady wants you out of this place."

Seven: Home Again

There are three schools of magic: Witchcraft, Shamanism, and Wizardry. The Witch draws her power from Elethay, and the power is abundant, but only within the will of the Goddess. The Shaman draws his power through spirit allies, and his power is limited by the power of those allies, and by his ability maintain those alliances. The Wizard draws power into the world by the strength of his own will, and at the cost of his own health; of the three, he is the most free, and the most limited. Of course, the Wizard can always choose to go down the dark path of the Necromancer, and deliberately cast unbalanced spells. This leads to great power, but also pours Warp into the world like a cancer.

—Dennold the Sage, "Introduction to the Arcane Arts"

I had a few moments to think while Chalice recovered from her shock. I tried to remember everything I knew about the temple and its layout, and did my best to come up with a plan that didn't involve Chalice being consumed by Clytemnestra. It didn't occur to me that Chalice might see the problem as much bigger than it really was…

"Quill, where can I go? They'll come looking for me, even if they don't know I'm a shapeshifter!" There was so much pain in her voice it hurt ME to hear it.

I did my best to sound hopeful. "There is a small Valarian enclave across the river; they'll take you in. They took me in, and I've told them all about you. All we have to do is get out of the temple, and cross the river. And the ferryman is my friend, so the river shouldn't be TOO hard."

"You're a Valarian?"

I shook my head. "Only an apprentice. And they tell me I'm also a dragon, but I haven't seen any evidence of it." Chalice stared at me wide eyed; I set her on the bed and started to take off my clothes. "There really isn't much security here, is there? They keep the girls in line by fear?"

Chalice nodded. "They say they'll kill us if we try to escape. And they will."

"Only if you get caught. And they are going to kill you anyway, if they find out what you are. So… We are going to do our best to disguise you as a farm boy on his way home from his first big night on the town." Chalice looked at me skeptically. "I'm serious. We use one of these scarves to bind your breasts, we use my belt pouch to thicken your waist, and you wear my clothes, including the boots. We go out the little door I left by last time, where there's only one guard, and we make sure he doesn't look too closely at you, because he will be dealing with the drunken orc in the yellow silk diaper."

Chalice giggled at that. "Are you that good an actor?"

I shrugged. "Who knows? I'm pretty much hoping the costume will carry the day. Do you have any alcohol around? The smellier the better. Don't worry it it's poisonous; I'm an orc, remember?" Chalice just shook her head, but she smiled as she did it.

We pinned Chalice's hair to the top of her head and made her a hat out of a piece of blanket, then held the whole mess together with the "Kanchaka" brooch I had brought back from Blackwater. When we were done, Chalice may not have looked a convincing farm boy, but she wasn't very convincing as a beautiful woman, either. I hoped that would be enough.

The escape from the temple went flawlessly; I staggered around a corner, tripped into the guard, and grabbed him above his waist so that I could hang on him with all of my weight. Chalice walked past and coughed, "Good night," at the guard as he was trying to get enough leverage to throw me into the street. We ducked into an alley, Chalice gave me back my trousers and boots-my shirt came to mid-thigh on her, and was as good as a tunic-and we made our way to the river.

The ferry was floating in mid-stream; I looked closely and identified a lump that I hoped was a sleeping 'Bacco. I threw a small rock at the lump; it stirred, and acknowledged my presence with a many-toothed grin. I heard Chalice gasp and begin to whimper behind me; I turned to see what had gone wrong.

"What... What is that THING?" she stammered, and I realized that the gods had one more trick to play on me before the sun came up.

"That's my friend Tobacco. He's a vermite. He's going to take us across the river."

"He's a RAT!" Chalice shrieked, and I clamped a hand over her mouth.

"He's my friend, and a good person, and your life depends on calming down and crossing the river with him. Understood?" I stared into her eyes, and she relaxed a bit. "How about this: Close your eyes, and I'll carry you." She nodded and closed her eyes; I took the hand off of her mouth and lifted her in my arms as 'Bacco brought the ferry to the near pier.

We were in mid-river when I looked up and caught the glint of 'Bacco's toothy grin. "You have a comment?" I growled.

'Bacco shook his head and continued to grin. "The last time you went to the temple, all you got was a good night's sleep. This time you're bringing home one of the girls. You still haven't gotten it RIGHT." He went back to grinning as I fought to suppress my laughter; Chalice opened her eyes timidly, and I lost the battle. I doubt that she found my laughter reassuring, but that was part of the joke.

I installed Chalice in my bed, and crawled off to try to grab a few hours of sleep on the smithy floor; I underestimated both my fatigue and Perrin's sense of humor. Perrin opened the smithy as quietly as he could, and then got out his heaviest hammer and hit the anvil with all of his considerable strength; I didn't quite bounce off of the ceiling.

"Your first day back after two months, and you can't even manage to stay awake. I'm ashamed of you, Boy," Perrin growled. I growled back, and got on with the day.

That evening we removed Chalice's Haskalad and Jikadell slave brands, which was a horrible process. I held Chalice's hands and provided moral support while Perrin and Jasmine alternately cut away the scarred skin and cast healing spells. When they were done, Chalice had severe but meaningless scars on her shoulder, which Jasmine assured her would fade every time Chalice shifted shape. Jasmine gave Chalice a strong sleeping draught, and I went off to spend another night on the smithy floor.

I dreamed that night. I saw a Farillan girl, who I knew was a unicorn, talking to a tall Ebonese man, who I knew was a necromancer. I seemed to be watching them from a great distance. The girl was asking for help, and did not know that the man intended to kill her and drain her soul. I tried to call out a warning, but could not make a sound; I tried to run to help, but could barely move. The necromancer turned and looked at me; he seemed puzzled by me, but my presence did not stop him; he reached out to cut the girl's throat...

I was sitting on the floor of the smithy and gasping for breath. As I shook off the effects of the dream I realized that someone was watching me from a few feet away. I peered into the gloom and recognized Ghost, the boy I had seen in the temple. My right hand slid across the floor to my dagger hilt as I summoned the friendliest voice I could manage and said, "Hello."

The boy stared at me for a while longer, then asked, "They're Valarians? The smith, and the shopkeeper?"

I thought about that. "What makes you think that they might be?"

"You told Chalice you were going to take her to stay with Valarians."

I tried not to gape; I hoped he couldn't see my face very well. "You were there?"

"The walls told me," he said, as if he were talking about something he had overheard in the marketplace.

"Ah. I guess that makes you a gargoyle," I said; he didn't answer, or even blink. "Yes, they're Valarians. Why don't you come back in the morning and introduce yourself? I'll tell Perrin to expect you."

He blinked once or twice, slowly, then nodded and faded into the darkness. I wrapped myself in my blanket and curled into a very tight ball to try to sleep, holding my dagger by its sheath like a talisman.

Ghost walked into the smithy the next morning as promised, and Perrin greeted him like a long lost nephew; in the afternoon Chalice surfaced with her hair and complexion dyed to make her look like a Haskalad.

Life settled into a quiet routine for several weeks. Chalice helped Jasmine with whatever needed doing; she was almost as wary of Perrin as she was of

64

the male rats, though she soon warmed to Pepper for some reason; it seemed that I was the only male who had been absolved for her ordeal in the Jikadell temple. Ghost watched and listened in the smithy, and generally wandered about; he spent as much time questioning rocks as he did talking to the living, and when he did speak, it was usually only to me or Perrin. I continued to learn smith-craft. Every few days 'Bacco and I crossed the river to visit Philo and collect free drinks from Stragus; the girl he had been obsessed with had disappeared, and he was inconsolable. Occasionally Perrin even joined us, though his dislike for Stragus and his disapproval of Philo were barely masked.

One evening I was sitting on the riverbank a few hundred yards north of the smithy; there was a rather comfortable stone outcropping there, and the river bent so that you could ignore Lechmore completely if you wanted to. I heard Perrin hobbling up behind me and turned to watch him approach, then offered him the best seat; he took it.

"Why don't you get that fixed?" I asked.

Perrin scowled at me. "Because it's proof that I'm NOT a gargoyle, idiot. It's just part of the job."

"You cut off your leg…"

"No, it was crushed by a taur cart. In public, in broad daylight, in Lechmore. And the DAY I decide to leave, you can bet I'll go into a stone trance and grow it back. But for now, it's part of the job." He shook his head sadly.

"And what exactly IS that job, Perrin? You hate the Haskalads, and yet you live on their doorstep." I sat on the grass facing Perrin as I spoke.

"Because someone has to keep the door open," said a voice off my elbow, and I turned to see Ravin; I forced myself not to jump, and Perrin grinned at my

65

efforts, then pointed across the river.

"There are about a quarter million people in Lechmore District, nearly half the people in the whole valley. Every year, about fifty of them find out that they're shapeshifters. About a dozen each of Morovians, unicorns, and wolves, plus a few each of dragons, gargoyles, pegasai, and werecats. There are about 500 necromancers, including apprentices, plus about 5000 mixed lackeys, all looking for those 50 confused kids. And against those 5000 troops, there are about two dozen Valarians, living VERY quietly, trying to get to the fledglings before the necros do. And they manage to get about half of them, and they send them to me, and I send them over the mountains." Perrin took out his pipe and began to fill it.

"Only half? So you're always looking for more Valarians?" I asked; I heard Ravin chuckle.

"Not really. At least, not for Lechmore," Ravin said. "Perrin can always use good people, but this is a stable situation; this operation is as big as it can get and still survive."

I didn't see it. "What do you mean? You can't rescue more than half the new shifters?"

Perrin shook his head. "Morovians and unicorns are free for the draining to any necro who can catch them; they're too hard to hold. Pretty much the same goes for gargoyles, though they're rare enough that it isn't a law. But the others are legally the property of Countess Cassandra Lechmore, Clytemnestra's older sister. And she owes twelve of them, including any dragons captured, to Bane. A few years ago we got ambitious and rescued 34 fledglings; Bane only got seven shifters in his tribute."

"And the problem with that was?"

"There was a crackdown. The next year we only rescued ten fledglings, and we lost eight of our own people, including two who sacrificed themselves to make Bane think our operation had been crippled."

I closed my eyes tightly and bowed my head. "Grey lady." Ravin raised an imaginary glass in tribute; Perrin just shook his head.

Perrin broke the silence. "We can do whatever we want, as long as we stay out of sight; the necros don't miss shifters they never knew existed. But once the necros have their hands on someone, all we can do is watch, unless we want to lose everything. 25 Valarians can save 25 shifters a year; it would take about ten thousand Valarians to save the other 25."

"But that would end Bane forever, wouldn't it?" I asked.

Ravin chuckled again. "Now THERE is a happy thought."

Perrin shrugged. "I think so. But the supply of necros is pretty much unlimited. It would be nice to see the whole valley as peaceful as the Ebonese district, though." I nodded, and Perrin continued, "I've enjoyed your company, Quill. But the day is going to come when I chase you across the ridge; they need warriors in the Manilac district a lot more than we need you here. And you don't seem too well suited to the ambush and murder work that 'Bacco and Whisky do to make sure the Haskalads are afraid of these woods."

I nodded again. "Probably not. But that day isn't here yet, is it?"

Perrin grinned. "Not yet."

"Well, then…" I shrugged, turned my back to the rock, and watched the light fade from the plains of Lechmore.

A few days later the storm season announced itself with an unusually large and virulent dragon storm; our little community gathered in Jasmine's store and rode it out in style. The following day Ghost came bounding into the smithy at a dead run. He made it obvious that he wanted to speak to me at the first opportunity. 'Bacco ambled into the smithy, and the customer with whom Perrin was dealing finally left.

"They've got Stragus," Ghost gasped. "And Philo. Stragus is a wolf; he changed during the storm yesterday, in front of a crowd of people. And when Clytemnestra went to gloat over him, he tried to buy his way free by telling her that Philo really belonged to Sojourner, so she sent guards to collect him, too. They're in the temple, now, but they'll be shipped south to Bogtown the day after tomorrow."

Perrin shook his head sadly and 'Bacco swore under his breath. I clenched my teeth closed my eyes. Ghost stared at all of us.

"Aren't they your friends?" Ghost asked.

I looked at him. "Can you take on 'Bacco in a straight up fight?"

Ghost looked at 'Bacco and then looked back at me. "No... Oh. Is it that bad?"

"At least," 'Bacco answered, and ambled off to the ferry muttering to himself. Perrin and I went back to work, though it didn't do us much good; everything we tried seemed to suffer from too much strength and not enough precision. We closed the smithy early, and I commandeered Jasmine's few precious maps for the evening.

That night I dreamed again of the necromancer and the unicorn girl; this time I saw him cut the girl's throat and begin the death drain ritual, but I crushed his windpipe before he could finish the spell. I woke up in total darkness; I set my back to the wall and ground my teeth for a long while before I went to sleep again.

I awoke again long before dawn, lit a candle, and began to pack the things I would need; when I was done, I found Ghost and explained my plan to him, then went to open the smithy.

Ghost came in with a pack ready, and Perrin followed a short time later. Perrin looked at Ghost, and at the pack that leaned against the wall near him, and looked at me expectantly.

"I'm leaving," I said. "I don't see much choice in the matter. I'm returning the great sword you made for me; it should nearly cover the cost of the hauberk and shield that I am taking. And this should cover the rest," I dropped my purse on the anvil. "I don't expect I'll need it."

Perrin shook his head. "I assume you have some kind of plan?"

I nodded. "I'm going to wait for the caravan to make its last camp north of the fork in the road that leads to New Mercer. Then I'm going to provide a distraction, and Ghost is going to set the idiots free. And I'm going to do my best to see that Dyson Brickwall gets blamed for the whole thing."

Perrin was skeptical. "What kind of distraction?"

I looked down, and grinned weakly. "I'm going to challenge the caravan to a duel."

Perrin gaped for a moment, then said, "It might work. How are you going to escape?"

I looked into Perrin's eyes, and saw that he already knew the only possible answer. "I'm not. But it's the best of several bad choices."

Perrin nodded and offered me his hand. "Go with the Lady's favor, Quill. Give my regards to Valaria."

I nodded, turned, and walked to the ferry; Ghost nodded to Perrin and followed me.

Eight: Martyrdom

If you get caught in a dragonstorm, things happen to you. You might get the Tox, and develop a warp feature or two. Or six, for that matter. You might shift. If you're human, you'll probably turn into a werewolf, though you might be a gargoyle. If you're an elf, you'll probably be a unicorn, or maybe a pegasian, though you might be a werewolf. Dwarves become gargoyles, Tigreans become werecats, Foxfolk become werewolves. And pretty much any of them might be a dragon. Necromancers look on warpspawn as potential slaves, and shifters as potential food. Valarians think warpspawn should be healed or killed, if healing isn't an option, and they see shifters as potential allies. Either way, you're better off with the Valarians. And of course sane people just stay as far away from the whole mess as they can.

—Leod, the Storyteller of Freepost

If you ever find yourself inclined to commit martyrdom, I have some advice.

First, get it over with quickly. Do not, for instance, give yourself three days to think about the situation.

Second, if you MUST delay the event, do it in prison or some other situation where backing out is not an option. Do not, for instance, put yourself in a position to have to walk for three full days lest you be late for your own execution, with nothing but your own will to keep you going.

Third, if you MUST take the long walk, do not saddle yourself with a companion who will question your motives whenever you get your own mind to stop questioning them.

Finally, if you MUST saddle yourself with such a companion, try to make sure that his survival is not critical to the success of your own mission, so that you can at least have the satisfaction of strangling him at some appropriate juncture.

The plan was simple enough; we had a day's start on the caravan carrying Philo and Stragus, and all we had to do was stay ahead of it until we reached the fork in the road that led to Brickwall's New Mercer, then turn around and make our play the next time the caravan made camp. This meant that we had to walk for three days before I would have a chance to commit noble suicide. Three days of intermittent conversation with Ghost.

"Quill," he asked at one point. "Didn't you say that Stragus was a brain-damaged bully? And that Philo was as deep as a mud puddle?"

I looked at Ghost and kept walking. "Maybe. What difference does it make?"

"Well… You're expecting to get yourself killed rescuing them."

I thought for a moment. "Why are you here? You might get killed, too."

Ghost shook his head. "Only if I get caught. And I won't. But you're not just taking a risk, you are committing suicide." He paused a moment. "And I guess that I'm here because you asked me to come."

I smiled. "Well, then, I'm pretty sure that they would have asked me, if they had had a chance."

"But you don't LIKE them!"

I sighed. "I like Philo well enough. I'm not sure it's possible to DISLIKE Philo, when it comes to that. Even if I do think he is an idiot much of the time. And Stragus… I keep thinking that Stragus might have been a decent person, if he had had any chance at all. It isn't his fault he was raised by sadistic sybarites."

"What?"

"Creeps."

"Oh."

I smiled again, and then shook my head. "But beyond that… If I let those two die, I am going to have to live with the knowledge that I could have done something and didn't for the rest of my life. And that the only reason I didn't help them was that I didn't want to. And not wanting to isn't a good enough reason."

"But no one else is doing anything."

"No one else is available. 'Bacco would be too easy to trace back to Perrin."

"I mean from Lechmore."

I laughed. "More creeps."

"Oh."

He didn't stop thinking about it. At another point he asked, "We have a day's head start. Why don't we set up an ambush? That might give you a chance to survive."

I nodded. "It might. But it also would mean that no one in the caravan would have a chance to back out." Ghost gave me a puzzled look; I continued. "If you are a merchant, or a driver, or a guard, you may not be working for the necros at all. You may just be in the same caravan. I don't want to kill anyone just for being in the wrong place at the wrong time."

"Even if it means you get killed?"

I chuckled. "ESPECIALLY if it means I get killed."

Ghost rolled his eyes and went back to thinking about it.

Eventually we reached the cut off for New Mercer. It was not quite noon; we backtracked to a likely spot and had a sort of odd picnic until mid-afternoon, then started marching toward home. The sun set and we continued walking; we saw the fires of a camp ahead shortly after full dark,

"VERY nice timing," Ghost whispered with a grin.

I shrugged and grinned back. "Just logic."

I waited with Ghost's pack while he made sure we were at the right camp. He returned quickly.

"It's them," he said. "Six wagons, about a dozen people." He drew a circle and a line in the dirt to indicate the position of the road relative to the camp. "The cages are on a wagon here, and there is a fancy tent that I guess is the leader's right here. So if you come in here, and I come in from here..."

"Looks good," I answered. Ghost helped me put on my armor, and I tried to go over his instructions one more time; he kept interrupting me. "And even if Stragus absolutely refuses to do what you say, keep after Philo..."

"He'll behave if I drop your name often enough. I know. Philo first, then Stragus, don't let Philo run until Stragus is free, fly across the river, and then turn north. It isn't a problem, Quill, really it isn't." He stepped back and looked at me. "I think you're ready."

"Not quite," I answered. I drew my dagger and gave it to him; it was the gilga-clawed dagger that Perrin had made for me. "I'm not going to need this, but you might. Remember me from time to time."

Ghost stared at the dagger for a long moment, then nodded and tucked it into his belt. "Give me a thousand," he said, then turned and faded into the night. I leaned back against a tree and started to count.

It was a good moment; I was at peace. The doubts were gone, and everything was going according to plan. All that remained was a short walk, and then a final flurry of violence.

I finished counting and began to walk; 500 steps later I found myself on the edge of the camp.

"Who is your leader?" I bellowed, much to the dismay of the sentry. "I have come in the name of Dyson Brickwall to claim the shapeshifters which are his rightful tribute." There was much scurrying about; a thin man stormed out of the pavilion, pulling his robes over a bare chest as he approached. His companion followed a moment later without bothering to find clothing; she was yet another multiply warped elf whose short brown fur, oversized ears, wings, and oversized claws formed a remarkably cohesive whole.

A Haskalad soldier faced me. "Who are you, and what do you want?" he barked.

"I am the emissary of Brickwall, and I have come for the shifters," I answered, loudly enough for the approaching necromancer to hear.

"You're WHAT?" the necromancer shrieked. "Stand back, everyone. Get away from him." He followed his own advice; when I was surrounded by a 20-foot circle of bodies, he turned to the warped girl. "Precious," he said. "Kill him."

I barely raised my shield in time to meet her first attack; she was that fast. She was also very strong, and her claws dripped poison. Fortunately, she had no martial skills to match her gifts; she was quite happy to catch every shield fake I threw at her, while I chopped away at her. My fourth strike broke one of her wings, and her master ordered his other bodyguards into the fray.

The bodyguards were typical Haskalad warriors; big, fast, and well trained. I did my best to concentrate on "Precious" anyway, and trusted my armor to deal with the other two. It was almost an effective tactic.

The four of us danced for quite a while; I acquired a number of minor wounds, none of them serious enough to matter; I wore "Precious" down steadily, in spite of her master's efforts at healing her. Eventually I landed an overhead smash that took off her ear, a piece of her skull, and broke her collarbone. She staggered backward and I expected her to settle to the ground, but she shook it off and charged back again. If I hadn't already been planning to die, it would have scared me.

I dodged away from the Haskalads and landed a perfect death thrust, just below the breastbone and rising to the left. Again she staggered back, and again I expected her to go down and stay there.

She didn't. She stepped back, coughed up blood, shuddered, and attacked again; a feint toward the Haskalad on my left turned into a full strength backhand swing off my right shoulder that caught her perfectly and took her head off.

I shifted so that one of the Haskalad's would have a chance to trip over her body, and grinned just a bit when one of them did. I heard the necromancer shrieking in the background, and suddenly I had several new playmates.

I concentrated on the Haskalad warriors; the teamsters that the necro had bullied into the fray didn't matter. By the time the first warrior had fallen, I was exhausted; my maneuvering consisted of little more that a quarter turn to the left after every blow fell. I had been hit more than a dozen times, but never seriously.

The second warrior fell, then a teamster, than another, then another. The footing went from bad to horrible; I took more cuts. My mind retreated inward, and waited sleepily for my body to accept the inevitable and get on with the business of being dead. And then I ran out of foes, and I found myself blinking in the firelight and sudden silence.

I heard a shriek, and saw the necromancer charging at me with a spear he had taken from one of the fallen teamsters; I cut him up unconsciously, as if I were practicing a sword drill. And then the silence returned.

I was alive. I was bleeding from an even twenty (by later count) sword, spear, and claw cuts; the claw cuts burned from some sort of warpspawn poison. I cleaned my sword on the necromancer's robe, then staggered to the wagon that held the cages.

The cages were empty; there was no sign of Ghost or the captives. I leaned against the side of the wagon and bowed my head in exhaustion while my mind tried to deal with the fact that I was still alive.

The poison saved me. I might well have stood there until I had lost enough blood to die in fact, but the pain from the poison was so sharp that it brought me back. I woke up enough to strip off my armor and clean my wounds, and then I staggered to the necromancer's pavilion and collapsed into his bed.

The next day I recovered my pack and then loaded the camp back into the wagons, bodies and all. I kept one wagon, the cages, and the necromancer's matched horses for my ride home, along with the better half of any valuables

I found. I made sure that each corpse had at least a few coins in its pockets; I would have hated to have the slaughter mistaken for a robbery. When all was loaded, I hitched up the taurs and set them ambling down the road toward Bogtown. That done, I hitched up my newly acquired horses and headed back to Ferrypoint.

Two days later, I stopped well south of Lechmore and made camp out of sight of the road; in the small hours of the morning I made a fire and broke camp, then drove north. At the first sign of dawn I entered the town and made my way to the waterfront; no one challenged me. I watched 'Bacco board the ferry and cast off, watched him clank his way across the river. I drove my cart onto the landing stage and waited.

'Bacco didn't recognize me in the hooded cloak I was wearing; he made no comment on the lumpy cargo under the tarpaulin in the back of the wagon. He said, "50 Imperials to cross," with bored indifference.

I flipped back my hood and said, "But I thought I had a free pass, 'Bacco." 'Bacco stared at me open mouthed, then pulled the chain out of the way and waved me onto the ferry. I pulled up my hood and drove forward.

We were halfway across the river before 'Bacco managed to get control of his jaw. Once he did, he said, "You know, it just occurred to me. You didn't get this job done right, either." And then he gave me his best sharp-toothed grin. I did my best to stare back at him impassively, but the laughter started deep in my chest, and fighting it hurt more that letting it out.

Perrin complained about the damage that had been done to the shield and hauberk; Jasmine hugged me and wanted to get right to work on treating my wounds; Chalice scolded me for not saying goodbye, and Brindle bit me again.

They dragged me off for healing while 'Bacco rifled my stolen goods; Chalice shifted to unicorn form to treat the poison. And then they told me that they had still not had any word from Ghost or Philo or Stragus.

I wanted to get up and go hunting for them immediately, but was told I would be hamstrung if I tried. I agreed to spend one day and night resting, and Perrin said he would do everything he could to get Whiskey's help.

There was a storm of wolfsong off to the south right at sundown; Perrin had Jasmine, Chalice, 'Bacco and I gather in the store with weapons. "Something is coming," he said. "That was a warning if I've ever heard one."

The wolves arrived shortly after full dark: Light, Shadow, and about a dozen other wolves, running easily and taking turns harrying another wolf with ram's horns and broken and torn bat's wings. The warped wolf was terrified and exhausted, but did not look injured beyond its maimed wings.

Shadow knocked the warped wolf off of its feet right in front of us, then grabbed it by the throat in his jaws. Light stopped in front of us, looked us all over, then stood on her hind legs and turned herself into a werewolf.

"Keep him away from my wolves," she growled. "At least until he has learned some manners." The warped wolf transformed itself into Stragus while she was speaking. "The only reason we haven't killed him already is that I thought you might put some sense into him." She looked pointedly at me as she spoke, then turned to Perrin. "Can you cure him of the warp? It would help if he were not so ridiculous."

"I can try, Lady Light," Perrin answered.

She laughed at that. "Willow. My name is Willow. I have been trying to get that through to Hunter Rat for more than two years."

"We will deal with Stragus, Lady Willow," I said. "One way or another."

"Lady?" Willow laughed. "Hardly." She threw back her head and howled, then dropped to all fours and resumed wolf form. She howled once more, then trotted away; Shadow and the other wolves followed. We watched them leave in awed silence, then 'Bacco and I picked up Stragus and carried him into the store.

"I don't suppose there is any question of asking his permission?" Perrin asked no one in particular; all eyes turned to me.

I shrugged. "This is Stragus. If we're going to wait for him to figure it out on his own, we might as well kill him now." 'Bacco chuckled and nodded.

"All right, then," Perrin said, and cast a spell; Stragus's horns started to shrink and retreat into his head. Jasmine cast another spell, and the maimed wings started to do the same. Perrin cast a third spell, and Stragus's murky Haskalad complexion faded to Farillan hues. Jasmine indicated that Chalice should heal the wounds that the wings had left behind, but she shook her head and stepped to hide behind me; Jasmine did the healing herself with a puzzled look on her face.

We carried Stragus to an upstairs room, and I retreated to my cellar; Brindle promptly curled up on my chest and fell asleep. I had nothing better to do, so I joined her.

Sometime later I was awakened by a hand on my shoulder; Chalice crouched next to me with a candle in her hand; Brindle was nowhere to be seen. "Why did you save him, Quill? Why didn't you leave him with the Haskalads, or with the wolves?"

I sat up and stared at her. "Because he's… Gray lady, you're the one he was obsessed with. The one he beat every night for not being happy." Chalice didn't bother to respond; she just stared at me accusingly. "I didn't know, Chalice, but I guess I shouldn't be surprised…" I shook my head sadly. "By the Lady, Chalice, I'm sorry. I'll make it clear to him that things have changed. He'll learn eventually."

She was trembling; I took her in my arms and rocked her to sleep. I tucked her into my bed, and went up to sleep in the smithy. As I fell asleep, a thought drifted through my head: Stragus got a bed, Chalice got a bed, and I was sleeping on the floor. Four days after my failed martyrdom, and things were very much back to normal.

Nine: The Order of the Red Wolf

The first time the Prophecy came to Valaria, way back when, she jumped right into the middle of a bonfire and howled it out as loud as she could. She wasn't burned, but it did turn her hair, and when she was in wolf form, her fur, bright red. That may be one of the reasons she never gave up; every time she looked at her reflection, she got another reminder. Of course, most of the prophets didn't just give up; they tended to have mysterious accidents, but Valaria was too tough and too smart for that; the only assassin that ever caught up with her was Time.

—Leod the Storyteller of Freepost

I dreamed again of the wizard's tower; I watched as he cut the girl's throat, and then I was on him, crushing his body with my hands. Suddenly everything froze, and I found myself looking into the girl's eyes; she held her hands to her ruined throat and stared at me in confusion and horror as her life ran away. I realized that I knew her name: Tayma. I started to reach out to her and found that I still held the necromancer; I hurled his body out the window, and suddenly I was falling...

I awoke to the smell of pipe tobacco cutting through the perpetual charcoal haze of the smithy; Perrin's pipe threw just enough light to show a short, broad shape in his usual chair. I considered ignoring him, but wasn't given the chance.

"We need to talk," he said. "About a few things, I guess. I went looking for you and found a girl in your bed, and you here. What's that about?"

I sat up reluctantly, found a candle and started fumbling with my tinderbox. "It turns out that Chalice was the girl Stragus was obsessed with, back before I liberated her. Seeing him gave her nightmares."

"And she came to you for protection? That explains half of it." Perrin drew on his pipe, and his eyes were momentarily visible.

"She's been one of Jikadell's girls for about six years, Perrin. She's planning to be celibate for a long time, maybe forever. She doesn't quite hate men, but she is afraid of them; it's a lucky miracle that she trusts me." I struck a spark, and the candle flared; Perrin waited quietly. "And while I understand that, and while I would never do anything to hurt her…" I held up the candle and looked at Perrin across the flame. "My ability to deal with the situation calmly pretty much stops at my collar."

Perrin smiled broadly and bit his pipe to hold back the laughter. "Thought something like that." He took another long pull on the pipe. "What did you think of the wolf girl?"

"Light? Or Willow… I should give her the name she prefers. Interesting. She seems to live with the pack full time."

"She does. We started seeing her about eight years ago; I checked my records last night, and a girl named Willow went missing during a dragon storm at about the same time from a village a few miles north of Lechmore. I think she's been living as a wolf ever since."

"I thought her speech sounded a bit strange. Lack of practice?"

Perrin nodded. "Seems likely. Smart girl, though. Did you notice how she directed her words?"

"She told me to watch Stragus, and you to heal him."

He nodded again. "She picked you as the leader, and me as a magician. Just by looking us all over. Interesting, no?"

"But I'm not the leader, you are."

Perrin stared at me across the bowl of his pipe for a long moment. "I'm beginning to think you may have some residual head injury we didn't catch."

I didn't blink. "If you're saying what I think you are, I wouldn't make the claim, and you know it."

Perrin laughed. "All right, boy. I'm an organizer; people follow my instructions. And I'm a teacher; I'm YOUR teacher. But you're a leader. People will follow your orders. It makes a difference. And the wolf knew it."

I scowled. "Thank you, I think."

Perrin chuckled. "It's the truth, and as much a curse as a blessing. Which brings up the reason I went looking for you…"

"Stragus."

"Stragus. I don't really know him, other than that idiot duel with you. But I know his father, and I know what the wolf said. He is YOUR problem. Don't let him out of your sight, and do whatever it takes to keep him out of trouble, including slitting his throat. Understood?"

I started to gather my things. "Can I take him with to hunt Ghost and

Philo?"

Perrin shook his head. "He shouldn't march today, which means you're stuck here with him. You can both get lost in the woods tomorrow."

"You're sure I can't take him with? They're already two days overdue."

"Stay close today; don't tire him out. Take him fishing a couple of miles upriver or something. Besides… There's something going on tonight that I want you to be here for."

Perrin ignored my puzzled expression; I tucked my blanket under my arm and went off to finish my night's sleep in the doorway of the room where we had left Stragus. I woke up before he did, which made me wonder how long the wolves had run him before they left him with us. I resisted an urge to kick him, then thumped the doorframe and called, "Stragus!" He snapped to a sitting position and I threw him one of the tunics I used in the smithy. He pulled it on past his blinking eyes, and started to complain.

He didn't blame me, at least. I would have beaten him senseless and thrown him into the river if he had done that. He directed his complaints at every deity he had ever heard of, every dragon ever spawned, and a small but select group of wolves. He complained while I collected hardtack and jerky from Jasmine's pantry; he complained while I collected various minor gear from the smithy; he complained as we walked through the woods to a spot that had both decent fishing and decent lounging. Then he took a short nap while I taught a few small fish not to try to steal jerky from my hook.

Stragus woke up, stretched, and started to complain some more; I threw a fish into his face. That took him enough off guard to silence him for a moment; I decided I needed to wedge in a few words of my own.

"You are looking at this from the wrong perspective, " I said. "Your old life was gone beyond recovery the moment you shifted. Dead. Over. Poof."

"But the dragonstorm…"

"Dragonstorm my eye. It was a warp storm. The dragons don't cause the storms, they don't follow the storms, they don't LIKE the storms. Your father and Clytemnestra and Black Bane and all of the other necromancers release the warp that drives the storms. Complain to them if you like, but not too loudly; every one of them (with the possible exception of your father, but I wouldn't push it) would cut your throat and suck out your soul in a heartbeat. Don't think about the life that you lost, thing about the fact that you WERE one day away from being a soulless corpse, and now you have a chance at a real life."

Stragus scowled. "Life as a homeless pauper? You can have it."

I sighed. I considered saying many things; I also considered cutting his throat and throwing his body into the river. Finally, I said, "You're not homeless, and you're not a pauper. Where do you think you slept last night? Where do you think those clothes came from? And you're entitled to a share of the stuff I brought back from the caravan that held you. You're a trained warrior, and you're literate, so you shouldn't have any trouble making a living, once we get across the ridge to the west side of the valley.

"We're going across the ridge?" Stragus asked.

"Soon. Perrin says it's my party, and I have a few loose ends to tie up here before we go."

"What's to stop me from going home right now?"

"Your father might suck out your soul, for one thing. And unless he kept you under lock and key, Clytemnestra would be after you again in a matter of days, and then you would tell her how you were rescued… In other words, if you cross the river, we all end up dead. So you don't cross the river."

Stragus stared at me. "So I'm a prisoner."

"No, you're an idiot. And if you try to prove it, we will stop you." He growled a bit at that, but I continued. "Stragus, you've been a parasite, a nuisance, and an embarrassment your entire life. The only reason I bothered with you was I had this feeling that, if you got a chance, you might turn into a worthwhile person. And I even put my life on the line to give you that chance. Don't waste it."

Stragus glared at me, but made no answer other than to retrieve the fish from his lap and toss it in my direction. I retrieved the fish, bit off its head and flicked out the entrails, then did my best to pretend it was delicious. Stragus turned slightly green; it was actually pretty good compared to some things I had eaten.

I have occasionally wondered where that conversation might have gone if it had been allowed to continue; I'll never know. I was just finishing my fish when Chalice came running up. I heard her call out, and a feeling of doom came over me.

"They're back!" Chalice said breathlessly. "Whiskey and Philo and Ghost just came back to Ferrypoint!"

She hadn't noticed Stragus yet; he certainly noticed HER. It may have taken him a moment to see through the died hair and skin, but he should have known her voice. I offered Chalice some water; she drank greedily, and then we both noticed that Stragus was on his feet.

"YOU!" he bellowed, and I clenched my teeth. "You are MINE!" Chalice took one look and ducked behind me; she was trembling so violently she could barely stand.

"I'm not sure what you're talking about, Stragus, but it doesn't matter any more." I said. "Chalice is a free person, just as much as you are."

Stragus's eyes bulged. "I bought her from the temple, after she disappeared. I posted the rewards. She's MINE!"

I blinked, then blinked again. "You OPTIONED a runaway slave? That's sick, Stragus, even for a Haskalad. Got a real good deal, too, right?"

That stopped him for a moment. "Yes. What of it? She still belongs to me; I paid for her."

I shook my head. "Past life, Stragus. Your current society doesn't practice slavery. And the lady doesn't want anything to do with you."

Stragus glared at me for another moment, then charged. I let him tackle me; I thought that was the surest way to get clear of Chalice. I rolled to my feet, found I was facing a werewolf, and that feeling of doom doubled itself.

I remembered those triple blow salvos he had thrown at me during our cudgel duel, and did my best to just stay out of his reach until he wore himself out. I did a diving roll which got me the spear I had been using as a fishing pole, and then stepped right into a three blow combination that left me bleeding badly.

It was a strange experience; Stragus raked me with his claws, and time all but stopped. Stragus's follow through and the second claw rake took hours, but I didn't seem to be able to move at all; I was too busy thinking. I was pretty sure I could still take Stragus down, but then where would I be? If I killed him, it would be pure waste; if I just beat him senseless, I was fairly certain any chance of ever redeeming him would be lost. The second claw ripped into me, and I watched the third strike of the salvo plow through the air toward me. I realized what I had to do, the third blow fell, time reasserted itself, and we disengaged for a moment.

I kept trying to stay out of Stragus's way while he got tired, but I started talking as I dodged.

"You can't do this, Stragus. Like it or not, all shifters are family. And you don't treat family this way. You don't treat MY family this way. Now change back, and STOP."

Stragus made one more attempt at a combination, then rocked back on tired feet and thought about it. It was a near thing, but he looked at Chalice, then snarled and charged; he got a spear butt in the belly for his troubles. His next attempt earned him a nice roundhouse crack against the side of his head, which staggered him. I took a breath to start preaching again, and got another set of claw marks for my troubles.

I got angry. I faked a roundhouse cut to the belly; Stragus bought it, and I snapped the spear butt into his forehead like a giant blunt arrow. He staggered backwards and would have fallen, but came up against a tree. I swept his feet out from under him and laid the spear point against his breast.

"You don't want this life? Fine. Say the word and I will chase you right to the void. Or you can stop being an idiot, change back, and behave yourself. Your choice." Stragus's claws quivered for a moment, and I tensed; I wasn't nearly as much in control of the situation as I was claiming. And then Stragus was shifting back into his original form; I stood up and took a long, slow breath.

Stragus stood up unsteadily; I snagged his shredded tunic with the spear and flung it at him; he looked at me with distaste. "Tie the rags around your waist. I'm not the one who destroyed it." He snarled, but did as he was told.

Chalice approached me; I realized what she wanted and shook my head. "Heal him first," I said. She glared at me. "I don't care HOW you feel about him. Lady help us all, he is my responsibility. And I don't accept healing while my people are hurt." Chalice continued to glare. "Please, Chalice. You don't have to touch him; you don't have to forgive him. But I CAN'T let you heal me until you have dealt with him." Chalice nodded, and threw some healing at Stragus; I gathered up my gear, and we all started back.

By the time we got to Ferrypoint, Chalice had used all of the healing magic she had. I was no longer bleeding, though my clothing was torn and bloodstained, while Stragus was nearly naked and sported two black and swollen eyes. The gathering in front of Jasmine's store started to call out greetings, then stopped and stared.

"We FELL." I said. "In a HOLE."

Several confused glances were exchanged; Perrin nearly bit his pipe in half before he said, "I know that hole. Keep meaning to do something about it." Then he clamped the pipe in his teeth again, closed his eyes, and quivered with suppressed laughter. The rest of us got down to having a reunion.

Ghost was openly hostile to Stragus; Stragus had tried to lead their group as soon as they were across the river. Ghost had repeated my instructions as he had been told to do, and Stragus had taken off on his own. After that, Philo and Ghost had been hampered by Philo's inability to walk very far in bare feet. Ghost was contemptuous, and Philo was defiant; Chalice and Jasmine tried very hard not to laugh as they told their story; Whiskey and Perrin listened quietly, and 'Bacco just laughed whenever he felt like it. When they were done, Ghost threw a last scowl at Stragus, who surprised us all by responding with a quiet, "I'm sorry."

Ghost wanted to know how I had survived, and was less than satisfied by my answer. "I ran out of enemies before I ran out of blood. I miscalculated. I'll try to make sure I die, next time." Ghost still wasn't satisfied, but he did smile.

We spent the rest of the afternoon figuring out who was going to sleep where, and generally outfitting Philo and Stragus. The booty from the caravan helped; Jamine's generosity helped more. Evening came, and Perrin had 'Bacco and me close up the smithy and clear all of the debris, and much of the usual equipment, out of the area between the door and the forge; it made the place look empty.

It was fully dark by the time we had finished; I started to leave, but Perrin sat down on the anvil and shook his head to indicate I should wait. The side door opened, and in came Jasmine, Chalice, Whisky, Ghost, Philo, Stragus, and Pepper. Pepper had Brindle the cat in her arms. Perrin directed Philo, Stragus, Ghost, and Pepper to sit against the main door; 'Bacco and Whisky stood to Perrin's left, Jasmine and Chalice to his right. I realized what was happening and caught Perrin's eye, then looked at Chalice, then back again.

"Chalice is a Valarian?" I asked quietly.

Perrin actually looked a bit embarrassed. "We... sort of needed something to do, a few nights ago... when we thought you were getting yourself killed. It seemed right, somehow." He shrugged, and took a long pull on his pipe. "Everyone ready?" No one answered; he pointed at me with his pipe stem and said, "You. Kneel. There." The pipe indicated the center of the room; I knelt facing Perrin and the anvil.

Perrin cleared his throat and started. "We believe in the blood," he chanted, and then the four beside him joined in. "Born of ancient dragons, purified by vision, sanctified by rending, exalted by storms."

My turn: "Blood of the shifter, blood of the mortal, blood of the earth."

91

Six of us: "Blood unifies all." A pause. "We defy the warp and those who embrace it."

Me, again: "Tox bringers, land killers, the ones who poison magic."

Six: "Upon their bones, we remake the world; we rejoin the circle; we purify the land."

Perrin stood and put his hand on my shoulder. "Quill," he said. "By virtue of the trust that has been placed upon me, in the name of Elethay, and in the memory of Valaria and of all who have died for the cause, I name you a Champion of the Order of the Red Wolf." He shook my hand, lifted me to my feet, and then clapped me on the back hard enough to take my breath away. "'Bacco! Where did you hide that keg?"

And that took care of the formalities. Gifts, of a sort, started to appear: the greatsword I had left with Perrin before going south; the dagger I had given to Ghost before I attacked the caravan; a stack of eleven coins and an apology for tardiness from Whisky. 'Bacco produced a self lighting magic torch that had belonged to the dead necromancer; he said he thought it was mine by right, but wanted to save it for this occasion. Brindle spent most of the evening on my shoulder, trying to dip her tail into my beer. Whisky and Perrin were amazingly jovial, Jasmine and Ghost were exactly who they always were.

Chalice approached to offer her congratulations with a strange look in her eyes, and a lopsided smile. "I go two more words than you did," she said with mock smugness. "In memory of Valaria, and Quill..." I blinked a few times, and then Chalice's eyes filled with tears and she hugged me fiercely. "I am so glad we were wrong."

And then there was Pepper. She caught me at a quiet moment, pulled my sleeve for attention, and said quietly, "Can I ask a favor, Mister Quill?"

Mister Quill? I blinked at that. "Certainly, Pepper. What do you want?"

"Take me with you, when you go west?"

I blinked again. "Why, Pepper?"

"I'm not strong, like Whisky, or 'Bacco. I can't DO anything here, except breed more Vermites. I can't do anything to make the world better. But you can, and you will. And I thought that if I could make YOUR world a little better, well, that would be something. I can cook, and I can sew, and I'm good with leather…"

"Stop."

"But…" She was getting ready to cry, shifting from a forlorn hope to none at all.

"I didn't say, No, Pepper. I said, Stop." Pepper's eyes grew wide. "One condition: ask your brothers for permission, first." Pepper's face fell again; I shook my head. "I said, Ask for, not, Get. It's rude not to ask, but if they refuse, they're being rude themselves and we can ignore them." Pepper blinked a few times, then grinned enormously and scampered off. I looked up to see Chalice looking at me; she rolled her eyes and smiled.

The party eventually ended. Later, as I wrapped myself in my blanket and tried to sleep, I realized that I had put my life on the line for Philo and Stragus, and my payment was that I got to listen to them snore. I smiled; I could live with that.

Ten: Walking in Shadow

While it is certain that Necromancers do deal in the animation of corpses, this is not what gives them their reputation as "Death Mages". Shamans deal with the spirits of the dead daily. No, it is their fascination with, and dependence on Warp based spells that gives Necromancers both their name and their reputation. Warp is poisonous and hideously addictive, and corrupts everything it comes into contact with.

—Dennold the Sage, "Introduction to the Arcane Arts"

Once again I was in the wizard's tower, and the scene unfolded with relentless similarity. Tayma poured out her troubles to the necromancer; he said reassuring things to her, and then cut her throat. I was finally able to move and barreled into the necromancer; my momentum carried us both into and through a paned window, and then we were falling into the darkness...

And falling...

And falling...

I woke up with a start, and found myself wrapped in a blanket at the bottom of the sump on Blackwater moor. I was suddenly unnaturally aware that my armor and weapons were exactly where I had left them on the night I expected to die; there was no sign of my pack or supplies. I dressed and armed myself, and was not surprised to see that my blanket had now also disappeared without a trace.

I climbed out of the sump, and my last suspicion that I was in the real world vanished; a thin, gray light glowed from an empty sky. There was no trace of fog, but it made little difference; the light faded to nothingness within a few hundred yards. I turned through a slow circle, hoping to see something familiar, or at least meaningful, and found a single point of light in the distance. I paused long enough to realize that I could no longer see the entrance to my sump, and started walking toward the light.

As I approached I realized that my goal was a small campfire; soon I could see a figure crouched beside it, feeding it a steady diet of twigs and small branches. The fire-tender did not look up at the sound of my approach; I stopped at a reasonable distance and called a greeting.

The tender looked up at me with empty eye sockets in a face of dry white bone; I realized I was dealing with an animated skeleton, and flexed my hands in preparation of drawing my sword. The skeleton just stared, and fed another stick to the fire. I approached warily, then crouched on the far side of the fire; the skeleton did nothing. I warmed my hands briefly at the fire, and the skeleton still did nothing. I shrugged and stood; the skeleton also stood; there was a spear in its hand. I took a step backward; the skeleton jumped over the fire and attacked.

I dove backward, rolled, and came up with my sword in my hands and a fresh (though minor) wound in my side; the skeleton turned to face me, and I shattered it. I looked around, saw another campfire in the distance, and trudged off in that direction.

I soon found myself at starting at another skeleton, which was tending another fire. I held my sword ready, but otherwise followed the same routine as at the first fire. The pattern held; the skeleton did nothing until I started to leave, then attacked; I smashed it with little effort. This time I saw two fires on the horizon: the one I had come from, and the one I would no doubt go to next.

At the third fire I considered saving time by attacking the skeleton from behind, but thought better of it. It was clear I was not in my own world, and suspected that ambush would be a violation of whatever rules were in force. Instead I just circled the fire until I could see a fourth fire in the distance, and continued walking; I heard footsteps behind me, and turned to face the spurned skeleton. I gave it what I had given its fellows, and continued on my way.

At the fourth fire, I walked to a point opposite the tender, saluted with my sword, and took a step backward to a guard stance. The skeleton rose, spun its spear once, and then circled out to put itself between me and the next fire. We engaged, I smashed it, and I continued walking.

I followed that pattern from then on, though occasionally a skeleton would surprise me by getting in a fast first hit, or surviving long enough that I had to hit it twice. I found myself getting tired, and my various wounds were quickly becoming stiff and sore; I wondered if the end of the sequence would come before I was so tired that one of the skeletons managed to kill me.

I lost count. Not that it really mattered, unless you took into account that I was not in the real world, and didn't honestly know WHAT mattered. That thought didn't help my rapidly deteriorating mood as I reduced yet another skeleton to fragments. This one had to have made my tally at least three dozen… but I wasn't sure. And it seemed to be important.

The temptation to just bash the next skeleton in the head from behind was enormous, but I gritted my teeth and circled the fire to my usual place, then gaped in shock when I realized that the cloaked figure at this fire was not a skeleton, but Chalice. I dropped my sword as she stared up at me with blank blue eyes (But weren't Chalice's eyes green?). She stood; I opened my arms to hug her, and she punched me in the face with a strength I had never suspected.

Chalice prodded me back to consciousness with her foot; she was standing over me with my sword in her hands. "What did you do with my dagger, thief?" There was an odd accent in her voice.

I sat up carefully and shook my head. I realized that this woman, despite her resemblance to Chalice, had auburn hair. "Stormchaser?"

"I thought you were going to rescue me, and instead you stranded me here. There aren't even any RATS here."

I looked at her carefully. I was exhausted, wounded, and on the ground; she held my greatsword as if she were quite used to it; I was clearly at her mercy. I decided I didn't care very much, and leaned forward to prop head on elbows on knees. "I'm sorry. I don't know what you are talking about."

"The day I met you on Blackwater Fang. You used some sort of spell to banish me here, and then you stole the dagger. I can break through to the life-side where the dagger is, but only if I can FIND the dagger. And I can't."

My curiosity got the better of me, and I looked up. "And you summoned me here, to lead you back?"

"I don't know. I just know that I'm not ready for the void yet. There are brawls to fight and wine to drink and love to make. And I have been waiting for CENTURIES for the chance to taste just a small bit of mortality, and YOU STOLE MY DAGGER."

I sighed. "No, I didn't. I gave it to your niece, exactly as I said I would."

"My niece? My niece has the Alicorn? And you know where she is?"

"I know where SHE is. " I answered. "I'm still not sure where I am."

"That doesn't matter. You're still alive, and eventually you will return to your body. And I can follow you. And then..." She threw back her head and laughed with joy. "FREEDOM!" She fell to her knees and threw her arms in the air. "But first we have to get you home." She looked into my eyes. "Any ideas of how to do that?"

I couldn't help smiling as I shook my head. "That's what I was trying to ask you."

"Oh. How did you get here?"

"I have no idea."

Chalice scowled. "What were you doing?"

"I was sleeping. Peacefully." I did my best to leave it at that, but honesty triumphed over wit. "I was having a nightmare, and I woke here."

"Probably you just need to fall asleep here, then. And THAT will be easier if you aren't bleeding..."

That sounded reasonable; I nodded and she helped me get out of my armor, then she shifted to unicorn form and touched her horn to each of my wounds. When she had finished, Chalice shifted back to her elven form and suggested something else that would pass the time AND put me to sleep, eventually.

I knew it was a bad idea, I really did. Sex with strangers is a bad bet; sex with ghosts is a worse bet. On the other hand, there was a naked woman in my lap who had just put three hundred years of pent-up enthusiasm into one kiss, and my ability to be rational about the situation was GONE...

I woke up in the real world, feeling warm and happy and vaguely delirious. In Chalice's room. In Chalice's bed. With my arms around Chalice. Calling the situation a bad idea was comparable to calling a glacier "A bit of ice."

I did my best to get out of bed without disturbing Chalice, made a hopeless attempt to find some clothing, and finally located and lit a candle. I was pulling on my trousers when Chalice looked up and smiled sleepily; her eyes were still blue.

"Stormchaser?" I asked hopelessly.

"Of course," she answered, smiling.

I clenched my teeth and nodded. "Put some clothes on. I'll be right back." Chalice smiled, shrugged, and rolled over to face the wall. I returned a few minutes later with Perrin and Jasmine in tow, and Chalice rolled onto her back and smiled up at us with sleepy blue eyes.

Perrin's voice was a bass growl that I felt in my stomach as much as heard. "I sure hope this was worth it, Boy, because this bit of stupidity is going to haunt you for a LONG time... IF I don't kill you first for GETTING ME OUT OF BED. ARE YOU INSANE?"

Chalice blinked a few times at that and sat up; I tried not to cringe and held my ground. "What color are Chalice's eyes, Perrin?"

Perrin squinted and said, "Blue"; Jasmine said, "Green," from memory. They turned and looked at each other in confusion.

"Perrin, Jasmine, may I present Chalice Stormchaser, Chalice Autumnleaf's aunt. The dead one." I felt an impulse to smile as the realization struck them, but I fought it.

Perrin bounced to the bed on his crutches and sat down; he grabbed Chalice's face in his hands and stared into her eyes; her eyes went wide in surprise and pain. After a moment he looked up at me. "All right, then, how?" he asked.

I shrugged. "I had the tower dream again, and fell out of it into… a spiritwalk, I guess. I think I managed to get lost on the spirit plane. I… Wait a minute." I picked up a candle and quickly examined my torso. "Here. This scar… It's from a wound I just got on the spirit plane, that Stormchaser healed."

Perrin kept a hand clamped on Chalice's jaw while Jasmine examined the wound; there were purple marks on Chalice's temples where Perrin's other hand had held her. "It's fresh," she said. "Cut and healing are both within the last couple of hours, and it has the feel of unicorn healing."

Perrin nodded and looked at me again. "Then what?"

I described the trail of skeletons and fires. "Every one of them had his back to me, and it would have been easy to start smashing them from behind… but that didn't feel right, and I would have taken HER head off if I had."

Perrin let go of Chalice's face. "So what's your story, girl? Why shouldn't I blast you out of that body you've stolen, and send you to the void where you belong?"

Chalice's eyes went wide, and she trembled. "Please. Please don't send me away. I will relinquish the body, and not return unless I am invited. I can help you; I can help her, my niece; I am much more of a warrior than she is. And I can make the full power of the Alicorn available."

Perrin nodded. "Then go. Give Autumnleaf her body back, and don't return unless summoned." Chalice nodded and went limp, then sat up and shook her head. When she opened her eyes again, they were green and hopelessly puzzled. Perrin took her head gently in his hands and kissed her forehead. "Quill has some things to explain to you, I think," he said. "Good night." He grabbed his crutches, levered himself to his feet, and he and Jasmine left.

I waited; Chalice just sat there looking dazed. Eventually I worked up the nerve to sit on the foot of the bed; I reached for Chalice's hand tentatively. Suddenly she sat up straight, then rolled over to rummage in her things on the floor beside the bed, then sat up holding the Alicorn dagger. It occurred to me that I should probably be afraid, but then I saw the wonder in Chalice's eyes.

"It talks!" she said excitedly. "I mean, she... I can hear her! Chalice Stormchaser is in the dagger!"

"Really." I tried to keep the apprehension out of my voice; I could imagine several things that Stormchaser might tell her, and many of them would do me no good at all. "What does she have to say?" Chalice just shook her head and said nothing in reply. She crossed her legs in front of herself, and then just sat there, staring at the dagger that she held in her lap. Occasionally she touched one of the bruises that Perrin's fingers had left on her temples and her jaw. I watched her, and worried.

I wondered just how much damage been done. Certainly my credibility with Stragus, and probably Philo and Ghost, would be shaken by this, if they learned of it. And my friendship with Chalice... She could accuse me of rape, if she wanted to. It wouldn't really be fair, or accurate, but it was possible. She could just refuse to forgive my stupidity, and that would be bad enough...

"That might be the most unhappy face I have ever seen," Chalice said softly. I looked up, and realized that the dagger was wrapped in the corner of the blanket; she was no longer holding it. She stared at me for a long time, then

101

finally said, "Did you enjoy yourself?"

"What? Um… Well… Yes, I guess I did. Does it make a difference?"

Chalice shrugged. "I don't know. You didn't mean to hurt me, and you didn't hurt me, really. And there is no one to whom I would wish happiness more than you, Quill. And yet I still feel betrayed." She shrugged. "Let's make sure it doesn't happen again, though."

"It won't. Not as long as I can remember what color your eyes are supposed to be." Chalice grinned softly at that, and I went on. "CAN it happen again? Can she just take you over like that?"

Chalice nodded. "Any time she wants to, if I am touching the dagger."

"Then we throw the dagger in the river."

She shook her head. "No, she is on her best behavior; she is afraid of Perrin, and promises she won't do it unless I call on her. But she did say that I should call on her if I ever have any more trouble with Stragus."

I thought about that, and smiled. "That could be interesting." I stood and turned to leave; Chalice picked up the dagger and put it beside the bed.

"She says to tell you good night, Quill."

"Well, good night to Stormchaser, then. And to Autumnleaf." I left, and closed the door behind me.

Brindle was waiting for me on my pillow, glaring at me suspiciously. I chuckled, then offered her the side of my hand, and she bit it, hard. I smiled and shook my head; Brindle wrapped herself in her tail and began to purr; I chuckled again, and got into bed.

I should have slept like a dead thing, all things considered. I didn't. My sleep was haunted by the image of the girl Tayma, lying dead on the floor of the necromancer's room with her throat cut. Her dead eyes managed to hold me and stare right through me; I was VERY glad of the dawn.

Eleven: Fire and Moonlight

It is not enough to see flight as a means of transport; lesser creatures have been doing that for millennia. We have taken to the sky; let us master it. We have found our wings; let us dance!

—Xart Oglevert, "Cyclopedia of Aerodynamics and Aerobatics"

I gave up on sleep and opened the smithy before dawn. I paused for a moment to stare into the forge, and suddenly Tayma materialized in the fire. I fell backwards out of my crouch, and then scuttled away; Tayma rose life size and burning in front of me, as if she had just ascended a stairway up from hell. Her expression was painfully sad and lonely as she reached out to me, then knelt at my feet and laid a timid hand on my leg.

"What do you want?" I asked. "What can I do?" And then I just stared mutely into her face until the pain in my burning leg made me jump and yelp; Tayma disintegrated into a shower of sparks and embers. I was forced to ignore my leg until I had policed the smithy for burning coals.

Perrin entered as I was cutting my trousers away from the burn; my hands were shaking from the pain. "That's a hand print," he said admiringly; I clenched my teeth and nodded. Perrin shook his head and began to rummage around until he had found some clean ash. He poured the ash over the burn, then cast a healing spell.

"What was the ash for?" I asked.

Perrin grinned. "So the scar will last longer." I growled at that, and Perrin just laughed. "So what happened?" I told him; he frowned and shook his head. "Sounds like you've got a ghost after you, or at least obsessed with you. Except that there is no way a ghost could exist around here without my being aware of it. And even if I DID manage to miss her, Ravin patrols the Spirit Plane where it touches this place pretty regularly..." He shook his head and sighed, then looked around the smithy. "Go bother 'Bacco for a while; I need to think about this."

I didn't quite do what I was told; 'Bacco was already in the middle of the river, sprawled against his windlass and looking for potential customers on the Lechmore side of the river. I sat down on a convenient rock— the same rock I had been sitting on when Stragus had "introduced" himself, so many weeks before— and watched Brindle lose a hopeless game of tag with a crow. It would peck nonchalantly at the ground, pretending to ignore Brindle while she stalked it, then flutter out of the way just before she was close enough to pounce. I admired Brindle's tenacity, and her optimism. It occurred to me that the crow would regret its audacity in short order if Brindle could fly, and suddenly...

It is difficult to communicate the process of spell casting to someone who has never studied wizardry; it involves complex mental contortions which are often dizzying and which many find impossible. As I watched Brindle stalk her crow, I realized that I knew exactly how to bend my consciousness in order to cause a pair of feathered wings to sprout from Brindle's shoulders. Suddenly the crow was off across the river at terror driven top speed, and Brindle was following, gurgling as she flew with demented joy. I grinned.

The crow soon recovered its composure, and put its lifetime of flight practice and habitual guile to work; Brindle had nothing going for her but energy and enthusiasm. The crow went into a slow, straight climb up the river course, deliberately letting Brindle catch up, then dove steeply toward the river. Brindle followed. The crow pulled out of the dive and shot across the river surface horizontally, inches from the surface of the water; Brindle, heavier and unskilled, went straight into the water.

I dropped the spell and hailed 'Bacco, telling him that he should intercept the strange disturbance that was drifting down the river toward him. He was puzzled, but complied; he was even more puzzled when he pulled an exhausted, sodden, and furious cat out of the river. He set Brindle on the downstream side of the ferry and started to crank his way home.

Brindle was still shivering when the ferry landed; I pulled off my shirt and used it to dry her off. 'Bacco leaned against the windlass and watched in bewilderment.

"You COULD NOT have thrown her from here to where she hit; it's more than a hundred and fifty yards. So how did the cat get into the middle of the river?" 'Bacco didn't like being bewildered.

"She flew," I answered; 'Bacco was unimpressed. I thought for a moment, and suddenly realized how exhausted I really was. But just possibly... "Follow me," I said, and carried Brindle, still wrapped in my shirt, into the smithy. Perrin was sitting on a barrel against the wall, smoking and thinking; he acknowledged our presence with one cocked eyebrow. "I think I can provide another piece of the puzzle, Perrin," I said. I closed my eyes for a moment to collect my thoughts, then stared into the forge.

Once again Tayma rose out of the coals; 'Bacco and Perrin both gaped, though Perrin quickly clamped his pipe in his teeth and pretended he had not been surprised; 'Bacco just stared.

"Perrin, 'Bacco," I said, "This is Tayma." The burning girl bowed to Perrin, and then to 'Bacco. 'Bacco pointed and tried to frame a question, but before he could say anything coherent, the burning girl shrank, sprouted wings, and turned into a cat. The winged cat did a lap around the smithy, then landed on the anvil. The cat's wings disappeared, and the cat hunkered into a sodden crouch. The effect was diminished by the fact that the droplets of fire ran up rather than down, but 'Bacco had just seen a sodden cat, and Perrin glanced from the cat on the anvil to the still soggy cat in my arms and made the connection.

"Fire Show spell," Perrin said quietly.

"As easy and low energy as they come," I continued. "I didn't know I could do the spell this morning when the ghost burned me, but it seems to have come back."

Perrin kept looking at me through hard eyes. "Do you remember anything besides spellcraft?"

I shook my head. "No. And I don't know much of that. I'm still feeling the effects of yesterday's escapades, and my mind feels like an empty barn. Though I seem to be more AWARE of my exhaustion, this morning; almost as if I have a better idea of what's missing than I did."

Perrin nodded; 'Bacco looked from one of us to the other and shrugged, then scratched Brindle on the head and ambled back to his ferry. Perrin continued to stare at me until his pipe burned out, then he set the pipe aside and stared into the forge. "I always thought that if I started to teach you the way of the Goddess— Witchcraft— that you might begin to remember your wizardry, Quill. And you approach witchcraft with a wizard's attitude. So the question is, how much DO you remember? Does any of it include necromancy? And can I still trust you?"

I glared at him. "I don't know any more than you do except for that last one.

And you should KNOW that by now."

Perrin smiled, but still didn't look at me. "Yesterday I did, Quill. But last night you betrayed a trust, and this morning you started casting spells, and now I'm not quite so sure."

"Oh," I said quietly. "That."

"That," Perrin answered, and looked at me. "Go rest. Figure out what really is in your head. And if there's anything in there that is going to hurt one of my people…"

"Don't come back."

"No, come straight back let me put you out of my misery," Perrin waved his pipe at the battle axe that hung on the wall; there may have been a trace of humor in his eyes, but I wasn't sure.

I retreated to my cellar, where I wrapped a blanket around my shoulders and sank into the restorative meditation that Perrin had taught me; Brindle disentangled herself from my shirt and began to preen the river out of her fur.

It was nearly midnight when I broke out of the trance; sleep would have been possible, but pointless. I considered putting on a shirt, and then realized that I didn't own one appropriate for what I had in mind; I grinned and made my way outside. There was a half moon rising over Lechmore, and it threw more than enough light for my purposes. I faced the rising moon, did some mental contortions, and felt a pair of feathered wings sprout from my shoulders. I took a few running steps, leaped, and was airborne.

I had done this before; I suspected that I had once been fairly skilled at it. I was absolutely certain that I had Oglevert's "Cyclopedia of Aerodynamics and Aerobatics" nearly memorized. I caught the small thermal over the forge and flew in tight circles while it carried me into noticeably thin air. I did one long, slow circle to take in as much of Kanchaka valley as I could see, and then started on Oglevert's exercises.

Natural fliers seldom do stunts; the instincts that let them fly tell them that inverted flight is a very bad idea. Magical fliers lack those instincts, and are free to indulge in all manner of stupidity, like wingovers and rolls and loops and stalls. It is truly glorious stupidity, provided one has made one's peace with the possibility of impacting the ground at terrifying speeds.

I felt the twitches of the spell expiring, and recast it in mid-air, then realized that I was not alone. Something— another humanoid flyer— was gliding toward me in a shallow dive from somewhere over Lechmore. I found the forge thermal and beat my way upward, suddenly aware that I did not even have a dagger on my person.

The other flyer continued to close; it was a bat-winged female, and I suspected that it was Sojourner's warped elf girl. She flicked her tail at me, and I felt a spike bite into leg. I fought an urge to panic; she had a ranged weapon, she had claws, she was a born flier...

No she wasn't. She was a warpspawn, and not a particularly bright one. It was a certainty that she had never heard of Oglevert... I went vertical and did a half roll as I was stalling, then dove straight into her. The impact startled her and killed her forward momentum. I punched her once in the face to disorient her further, then kicked away and tucked tight. My wingtips pulled me into a nose first dive, and I carefully opened my wings and leveled out. By the time I had turned and had a chance to look for the lizard girl, she was far below me, still tumbling helplessly as she tried to recover from a simple stall. There was more than one sharp crack as she hit the trees; plainly audible in the still night air. I tried to memorize the spot as I circled downward.

I took the time put on my leathers and arm myself before I went looking for her, but she was long dead when I found her; the fall had left her dead or dying. I was surprised to see a blonde wolf standing guard over the body, though. "Good morning, Lady Willow," I said.

Willow yawned and shifted to a more humanoid form. "I thought she had your scent on her," she said. "And that you would come looking for her, at least to see she was dead." I nodded. "What do you intend to do with her?"

"Weight her a bit and throw her in the river, probably. She belonged to a powerful necromancer, and the more we can confuse the manner of her death, the better." I looked at the dead creature, and could see the girl she had once been all too clearly. It made me sad, and angry. I started to lift the body, but Willow waved me away and threw it over her shoulder effortlessly.

"Old habit," Willow said with a lupine grin. "In the old days, I just automatically did any hard labor that needed to be done. They used to say that I was the strongest man in the village." She grinned again, but there were more teeth in it this time. We started walking.

"You were waiting for me, Willow?" I asked.

She nodded. "I need to leave this place, and I have heard that you are going to
leave soon, and take some people with you." I started at that, but she just shrugged. "I keep a closer watch on Ferrypoint than even the Hunter Rat knows.. They are good folk, and I miss being human sometimes. More and more lately; I am becoming less good at being a wolf."

We reached the river; at my instructions, Willow held the body underwater and squeezed the air out of its lungs and stomach, then let them fill with water. Once we were sure the body would sink, Willow pushed it out into the current, then climbed out of the water and shook herself thoroughly. I led her to the rock I had come to think of as "Perrin's Bench."

"You are becoming less good at being a wolf? What does that mean?"

Willow sighed heavily. "It means that I disrupt their order. Wolves don't like having a queen; it upsets them. There was a time when they needed me, but now that Shadow is full grown, he can offer them anything I can. And they want him to be their King."

"I am still not seeing the problem. Can't you step down?"

"Only if I am dead, or missing completely. So I want to leave." She shrugged. "Shadow's father was King when I joined the pack. When he was killed by drakkels, I took over the pack by force, and led them to war with the drakkels. And now Shadow is full grown, and it is his time."

I stared at her, and tried to understand. "He's your son. Shadow is your son."

Willow seemed puzzled by my confusion. "Of course."

It was my turn to shrug. "I did not understand just how thoroughly you had become a wolf. It makes sense now. Except… Why me?"

Willow snorted, and laughed as well as her wolf's face would let her. "I do not know my way outside of these woods. I need to follow someone. And I have been the wolf queen; I will not follow someone I do not respect. Who else is there?"

I scowled at that, then nodded. "The sun will be up soon; I need to get back and open the forge." Willow responded by shifting back to wolf shape and following at my heels.

Brindle was waiting inside the smithy; she took one look at Willow and hissed; Willow stared back placidly. Something transpired between them, and then Brindle climbed down and started to do an odd hopping sort of dance at my feet; Willow settled into a place in the sun with her back to the open door. I stared at Brindle.

"Do you want to fly, silly Cat? Is that what you're trying to say?" Brindle stopped hopping and stared at me expectantly. "Sorry, all out of wings for now. Maybe later." Brindle blinked a few times, and then started to slink away. "Of course, if you just want to practice landing, I could throw you in the river right now," I said under my breath; Brindle was already out of sight. I got on with my work.

A long stretch of hard labor later I noticed that Willow was still in her place by the open door, but now sound asleep. Brindle was curled up inside the circle of Willow's legs, sleeping with her head on Willow's paw. I closed my eyes and shook my head, but nothing changed. It was a pleasant, homey, restful scene— with overtones of significant madness. I stared for a moment while I considered the course of my life, then went back to my work

Twelve: Sundry Complications

If the day to day mechanics of running a war don't break your heart on a regular basis, it's not a war, it's just a gladiator show with really bad seating.

—Perrin Ironhand

Perrin didn't come back until I started to close the forge for the night; in the meantime, Pepper brought me two meals and spent a great deal of time staring at the yellow wolf that was nearly twice her weight. Eventually she took her cue from Brindle and made friends with Willow, all without any words being spoken. I just smiled, and tried not to get involved.

I was about to bank the forge when Perrin turned up; he told me to shut the doors and stoked the fire instead. He told me to sit on the floor and close my eyes, and keep them shut until he told me to open them; I obeyed. He puttered about for several minutes then set a stool between me and the forge, within easy reach of either. He settled himself, then stared to talk.

"There are several ways of going about this," he began. "But in the end, it all comes down to you and the Goddess. Either Elethay is willing to share her power with you, or she isn't. If she is, fine; if not... Well, that's what I'm here to find out. I have given you all the knowledge you need to practice Witchcraft, but the fact is that I still have my doubts about you." He paused, and I could hear the bellows creaking. "And I hate those doubts, because I

LIKE you, Quill. And my friends... my family like you. And as hard as I try, I can't find any hard evidence to say that I SHOULDN'T trust you. But... You used to be a necromancer, and you have somehow managed to be haunted by a ghost that no one on the spirit plane can see. So it is obvious that there is a lot about you that I don't know. You may not know either... but I have no proof." There was another long pause, and again I could hear the bellows working.

"So we are going to leave it in the hands of the Goddess. You are ready to be initiated, and she will accept you, or she won't. If she accepts you, I will trust her judgment. And if she rejects you... I guess I will just have to trust my doubts, and regret it later." Another pause, more bellows. "Hold your right arm out, Quill, straight from the shoulder, palm up, and keep it there until I say to move." I obeyed.

"Now, concentrate on the Goddess. Ask her to accept your service; make whatever pledge you care to make. Ask her for her protection. And wait." Again, I obeyed. I though of all that Perrin had taught me of Elethay; my arm began to get heavy and started to tremble. I thought of my meeting with Valeria on the spirit plane; I thought of all of the warp-created horror I had seen and heard of. I clenched my teeth in the effort to keep my arm extended, and then...

The voice came and was gone like an arrow in flight; I did not so much hear it as know it had spoken. A rich, smiling, female voice had said, "Patience, Grandson; let the dwarf have his fun." At the same instant, there was a feeling of intense heat and some weight in my open right palm. I waited for the pain that had to follow that much heat, but it never came. The heat grew less, and then was only a pleasant warmth.

"Damn me to the Void nine times over, Quill. I think that you passed this one. Open your eyes, but don't move your hand yet; you need to appreciate the whole scene."

Perrin was seated off to my right; his axe was leaning against his stool in easy reach. I realized that he had planned to kill me on the spot if I had failed the initiation. The forge was to his left; I saw a small crucible sitting in the forge. Perrin still held the tongs he had used to manipulate the crucible.

"Molten lead?" I asked.

Perrin smiled and shook his head. "Go ahead and look, son."

I reeled in my nearly exhausted arm and looked at the object in my palm; it was a bronze casting of intricate knotwork. "Why did you need the crucible for this? Why not just move it with tongs?"

Perrin just smiled and shook his head. "It was molten. What you have there is a piece of original sculpture."

I stared at the thing in my palm; there was no question it was beautiful. On the other hand... "You poured molten bronze into my sword hand, and were going to cut me to bits if I flinched?"

Perrin shrugged. "I've seen you fight, Quill. If I had to kill you I wanted make sure things went my way. You know how much I hate to gamble."

I growled and held up the casting. "Is this sort of thing usual?"

Perrin shrugged. "Damned if I know. I've never witnessed an initiation by ordeal before; I've only heard rumors. Usually initiations run more along the Valerian pattern."

My face went blank while I thought about that. "No more doubts, though?"

"No more doubts. By order of the Goddess." He scrounged a bit, produced a leather thong, and threw it to me. "Given its origins, you might want to keep that thing with you." He smiled as warmly as I have ever seen him do, and added, "I'm off… Supper will be ready when you finish putting this place to bed. The others don't know what I had planned tonight; they just knew that the forge was off limits. Tell them what you want." He smiled again, shook his head, and left.

I strung the medallion on the thong and hung it around my neck, then put away the tools Perrin had used and finally banked the forge. I kept stopping to examine the medallion; it had no trace of magic about it that I could feel, either as wizard or witch. And yet… I shook my head. I didn't understand, and knew I was not meant to. Somehow that was enough.

Chalice, Ghost, Stragus, and Philo were all gathered at Jasmine's table; 'Bacco, and Whisky were loitering over a table game that neither of them enjoyed. I didn't see Pepper, but I suspected that that was because she didn't want to be seen. Everyone seemed nervous; I wondered how Perrin had convinced them to stay away from the smithy. I pulled the medallion off of my neck, looped the thong over a finger, and then closed my hand over it.

"Where's Willow?" I asked. "She should be here." Pepper materialized momentarily with Willow in tow, which prompted Jasmine to make disparaging comments about wolves at her table. Willow shifted to a form that was human enough to make Jasmine object to the extent of Willow's nakedness, which prompted a scramble for appropriate clothing. Given that Willow was taller than Whisky and nearly as broad as 'Bacco, it was a fairly amusing scramble, during which Willow flashed me a covert smirk that let me know her innocence was a fraud. Once a sufficiently large cloak had been found and order restored, all eyes again returned to me.

"Is anyone familiar with molybdomancy?" I asked, and was answered with blank stares from all but Perrin. "You pray for guidance over a small quantity of molten metal, then pour it out onto a surface and try to take your answer from the shape the metal takes." I held my hand over the table and let the medallion fall to the end of the thong. "And so I have an initiation gift from the Goddess herself. Not bad, eh?" I swept my eyes around the room, and assured myself that Jasmine, 'Bacco, and Whisky had been in on Perrin's plan, whether they approved or not. I sat down and let Chalice take the medallion; she passed it to each of the others in turn. Once it had made the rounds, the food started to appear, and we had a VERY merry feast. I couldn't help but wonder what they would have done if I had failed.

Eventually the gathering began to break up; Willow reverted to wolf form and retreated to a corner in the company of Brindle and Pepper. Perrin, Jasmine, Chalice, and I were still at or near the table when Ravin appeared. Chalice was shocked; she had never met Ravin before. Jasmine and I were merely surprised; Perrin indicated that Ravin should join us at the table.

"I take it our orc passed," Ravin said with a smile. We all nodded, and I passed him the medallion. He examined it at some length, returned it to me, and then said, "I imagine this commits you to the next step, Perrin."

Perrin nodded and said, "I guess it does."

"The next step?" I asked.

Perrin nodded again. "We need to find your ghost, Quill. We need to find out what Tayma wants, and try to set her free."

"All right," I said. "Any ideas of how to accomplish that?"

Perrin and Ravin exchanged a glance, and then Perrin spoke. "We think you need to try to track her down on the spirit plane."

I scowled. "I thought you said that there was no trace of her on the spirit plane."

Ravin grinned. "On the surface of it, on that part of the spirit plane that is more or less tied to the physical world, no, there is not. But the planes are all more complex than that; remember how many extra layers being able to fly adds to the physical plane. On the spirit plane, every single person has a piece of it inside of them, more or less. Or at least there are sections that only that person can get to. The point is that Tayma is not getting at you from the outside, she is somehow trapped inside of you, and is trying to communicate, or escape, when your control is weakest."

I looked from Ravin to Perrin and back again. "And the reason you have so many reservations about this process, that you are trying to hide from me?"

Perrin shrugged. "The personal sections of the spirit plane; they are where nightmares live. Goddess only knows what you'll run into."

"You want to send me to a place where all of the garbage in my mind can take shape and do physical damage to me." I shook my head. "The molten bronze was just a warm up, wasn't it?"

Perrin smiled sheepishly; Chalice watched with increasing horror; Jasmine just listened. "I don't see that we have much choice, but there is one consolation: Ravin will be going with you," Perrin said. I didn't answer, I just stared. "We can build Ravin's participation into the ritual. The spirit plane is his home ground, now, and as long as your physical body is inside his boundaries, he should be able to follow you wherever you go."

"Stormchaser wants to go," Chalice said suddenly. "She says that if Ravin can go, the same rules should apply to her, as long as Quill's physical body is in contact with the Alicorn."

Perrin, Ravin and I exchanged surprised glances. After a few moments, I said, "I'm willing to be overruled, but is there any reason why we should

NOT let her go? She IS a battle-hardened unicorn, and she has knocked me off of my feet twice."

"Among other things…" Perrin muttered disgustedly. Jasmine giggled, Chalice clenched her teeth and closed her eyes in fighting a smile, and Ravin just laughed out loud.

I wasn't particularly amused; I said, "THAT is a closed book; if she can't control herself, she can always bother Ravin. The question remains, Why not?" Ravin stopped laughing and grew thoughtful; Perrin looked at him and tried to fight his own grin.

"She's right," Perrin said at last. "I can add her to the ritual with little trouble. And you could probably use her help."

"Probably," I agreed. "When do we do this, then?"

"Tomorrow at sunset? Spirit magic is always a little stronger after sunset, and I have never tried this trick before." I looked at Perrin when he said that, and he gave me the slightest of shrugs. "And you can use another day to rest, Quill. This may take a lot out of you."

"Or kill me?"

Perrin shrugged again. "Or kill you, but probably not. You're hard to kill. Now get some sleep."

At some point in the small hours of the morning I was awakened by Willow's growl; Ghost had tried to slip into my cellar and out again unnoticed, and had not been prepared for the man-sized wolf on the floor beside my bed. Ghost had had the sense to freeze in place and try to sort things out.

I made a light and stared at Ghost; he was holding a small, ornate harp.

"And the reason you're here?" I asked.

Ghost indicated the harp. "I couldn't very well give this back to Philo tonight; he would have caused a scene. I thought you could keep it."

"That's Philo's harp?"

Ghost nodded. "He's been mooning over it every since he was rescued. He talks like it's alive."

I shook my head. "You're a good friend, Ghost. Not particularly sane, but a good friend."

Ghost grinned. "I wanted to hear him play it; even 'Bacco says he's pretty good. And it was fun."

I kept shaking my head. "It has never even occurred to you that you might get caught, has it?"

Ghost thought for a moment, then grinned again. "I used to think about it; now I just make sure it doesn't happen. Besides, everyone in Sojourner's household is busy staying out of his way; he is REALLY angry about that flying girl." He gave me the harp. I took it and ran my fingers over the strings; it had held its tune surprisingly well, and I corrected the changes with little difficulty. Ghost stared. "You can play the harp?" he asked.

I thought about it. "I have studied, I think. I know how to tune it, and play a few basic chords." I shrugged. "Just another part of the mystery, I guess."

"You'll know tomorrow, though, won't you? After you free that girl from the spirit plane?"

"What are you talking about?" I growled.

Ghost sighed. "I listen. I hear things. Perrin talks to Jasmine; Perrin talks to Ravin; Perrin talks to you. Nobody much talks to me, but it doesn't matter." He paused to grin at me. "Perrin thinks that this spirit walk will bring back your memories, and maybe free your dragon. He's not really very concerned about the girl. But he doesn't want to send you over the mountains if you're going to turn into a necromancer; that's why he initiated you into Elethay before the spiritwalk. And he's STILL not sure, not really. He doesn't want Ravin to go with you, because he's afraid Ravin's spirit might be lost if they have to kill you."

I kept plucking random chords and thought about that. Finally I said, "You really are a good friend, Ghost. Go get some sleep; we'll talk more about this tomorrow." Ghost faded into the darkness as I continued to play the harp softly.

A short time later someone said, "You're still going to do it, aren't you? This hasn't changed a thing for you."

I looked up and saw that Willow was now humanoid enough to speak. "You're right," I answered. "This doesn't change a thing. Though it does make things make more sense." I looked up, and realized there was another question she hadn't asked. "Don't try to avenge me. If Perrin has to kill me, it will be the right thing to do. Your job... What I want you to do... is get the others safely to the Ebonese district on the far side of the valley, particularly Stragus and Philo. Chalice might be able to stay here, and Ghost will be fine wherever he chooses to be, but the other two will need your help."

"What if they don't want to follow me?"

"I'll make sure they know what I want done, and then you will have to beat Stragus senseless at some point; it's the only thing he really understands.

And here you thought you were done with being wolf queen."

Willow chuckled. "And now I may get to be werewolf queen. It's still better than plowing fields."

"I guess it is at that." I set down the harp, quelled the light, and slept until midmorning. Once I was up, I put together (or at least requested; no one would let me do any real work) a large picnic lunch, and led my strange little band off into the woods: three elves, a young human, an orc, a vermite, a wolf, and a cat, more or less.

We found a likely spot that was sufficiently remote, and then Ghost returned Philo's harp; Philo tried hard not to cry, and almost succeeded. Philo started to play while the rest of us ate; we had to threaten to take the harp away by force before Philo would eat anything. When Philo had eaten, we gave him his harp back and settled into a sated, sleepy sprawl.

"Philo?" said a surprised voice I didn't recognize; my eyes shot open wide.

"Shoglar?" asked Stragus with just as much surprise, and suddenly I was on my knees.

"Stragus? What the Void have they done to you?" asked Shoglar, and I was on my feet with my sword in my hands; Shoglar turned out to be a Haskalad soldier with two companions. Shoglar might have been present at my first duel with Stragus, but I wasn't sure; I had seen him a few times in Lechmore in Stragus's company.

"Hello, Shoglar," I said calmly. "My name is Quill. What can I do for you?"

"We're looking for Sojourner's lizard girl," Shoglar answered before he could sort things out. "Stragus, I thought Brickwall had you." I could see

Shoglar was trying to work out his position, and I suspected that he was getting an answer I wouldn't like.

I decided not to give him a chance. "I'll give you all of the answers you want after you lay down your arms and surrender. No point in educating you if we're just going to kill you."

I could almost hear Shoglar working it through: I was a problem, and Stragus was a problem if he fought, but he might not fight; Philo, Chalice, and Pepper were inconsequential; Ghost was not likely to be a problem. So it was really three to two, and maybe three to one… and then Willow rolled to her feet, looked Shoglar in the eye, and growled slightly. Shoglar's eyes got wider; he glanced back to Chalice, who responded by drawing the Alicorn casually and flipping it in her hand. Shoglar dropped his spear, and his companions followed suit.

"Damn," said a voice that wasn't quite Chalice's; I looked down and saw blue eyes glaring at me through a curtain of auburn hair. "I was hoping we were going to get to kill them."

I sighed. "They were raised to believe that shapeshifters were monsters who would hunt them down and kill them if they got the chance. If we had killed them, they would have been right. I had to find another way."

"Spoilsport," Stormchaser growled, and then her hair became lighter and her eyes turned green. I smiled weakly to acknowledge the change, and hoped that I was right.

Prisoners. Gray Lady help me, I had prisoners.

Thirteen: Necromancer's Nightmare

When I was a child I lived for heroic literature. I had three different versions of the tale of Kasalorn Kinsaver, and I had each nearly memorized. And now... I have become everything Kasalorn fought to prevent. Children are idiots, and I was no exception.

—Kelestor Sar, "Journal"

Kelestor Sar looked out over the sleeping city and thought about his love/hate relationship with the Haskalads. They had made him rich and powerful; their parties were marvelous, their slaves were fabulously well trained, and they all but worshipped warp. But for all of that, their petty cruelties and incessant political gaming just made him tired. It was time to gather up his possessions and find a place of his own. He didn't want much, really. A few square miles, a few dozen slaves, and isolation. But isolation was the great trick.

There was a warpstorm forming in the distance, and Kelestor thought that some lucky necromancer must have found a shape shifter to drain. He looked back at his borrowed bed, half expecting to see the slave girl sleeping there, but she had returned to her pallet at the foot of his bed once he had finished with her. He thought that she embodied most of both the good and the bad of the Haskalads: she was a nearly perfect servant; she was attentive, thorough, fastidious, and almost painfully eager to please. She even tried to give the impression that she enjoyed and took pride in her work. But if you looked into her eyes... There were wells of terror in her eyes, along with that constant plea: Please don't beat me; please don't maim me; please don't kill me.

He looked back out the window; the warpstorm was either much larger or much closer, perhaps both. He watched the lightning flash its unnatural colors across a sky that seemed to occasionally open onto the Void itself. He could just begin to feel the pleasant pulse of the warp in the pit of his stomach.

Of course, that reminded him of his great secret, the fraud that haunted his every movement among the Haskalads. They assumed that he was a master necromancer, just because he knew more spells than any of them did, just because he had learned the theory behind magic and not just a list of spells. But for all of his power, he had never drained a single shapeshifter.

The Haskalads assumed that he must have been a great power at home, because of his knowledge; they didn't know he had been driven from home in fear for his life when his peers had found out he was practicing warp magic. He had been given one chance to forswear warp forever or die, and he had chosen instead to abandon family and friends to take his chances with the Haskalads.

He couldn't give up the warp. From the first time he had twisted a spell into one of the permutations his instructors had specifically forbidden, he had been hopelessly addicted. It didn't matter how much harm it did to the world around him; it didn't matter how much it hurt afterward, and it frequently hurt a great deal. While the warp rush was on him, it was simply too wonderful for words.

He knew how to drain a shapeshifter, of course; he had long since worked out the intricacies of the death drain, and the month long ecstasy of the soul drain. He even was fairly certain that he knew how to make a soul gem in which he could store the stolen energy. But in the Celestial Empire, shapeshifters were protected from necromancers, and in the Haskalad Empire, shapeshifters were reserved for powerful nobles.

The storm was nearly overhead now; a bolt of green and purple lightning reached forward and hit the roof above his head. The building shook, and Kelestor was momentarily deafened by the roar of the instantaneous thunder. He felt a rush of warp run through him, and he grinned. As his hearing returned, he noticed odd sounds coming from the room behind him, and he turned to see a unicorn struggling to free herself from the wreckage of her bedding and rise to her feet.

He reached out a tentative hand and said, "Stop. Just relax, and try to shift back. Everything will be fine." He knelt beside the girl and tried to comfort her, tried to coach her to change back to her original form, tried to be as friendly and as helpful as he could. But even as he was at his most charitable, his mind was saying, "No one else knows she's a unicorn. She's a Haskalad slave; she's been assigned to you; as long as no one knows she was a unicorn, you can kill her for any reason you want, and no one will think twice about it." And the storm raged overhead.

The girl was back in her own form now; Kelestor helped her to his bed and wrapped her in the blanket. He kissed her forehead tenderly, and assured her that he would be able to keep her safe. Once they got through the sweep for new shapeshifters that followed every storm, he would buy her from his hosts (her owners) and he would take her away to a Valerian enclave that he knew about. And while he talked, and comforted her, he found his belt dagger and quietly drew it from its sheath. And the storm raged overhead.

He sat beside her on the bed and brushed a lock of hair out of her eyes. It was such a pity, really. She was a sweet girl, quite pleasant to look at, and she had tried so very hard to be good at the job that had fallen to her. Kelestor ran his hand up the back of her neck and knotted his fingers into her hair.

He shifted on the blanket and bent down to kiss her softly on the lips. Her arms and shoulders were pinned by his weight on the blanket; her head was held firmly by his hand in her hair. He looked into her eyes, smiled lovingly, spoke the key phrase of the death drain, and cut her throat.

Kelestor felt a warp rush that made all of the others fade to shadows; it felt so good that he was certain that he would explode from the pleasure. A second bolt of lightning hit the roof above his head, and suddenly he WAS exploding, and the pleasure to the point of pain had just become pain, and more pain. The girl's expression turned from horror to confusion just before her eyes glazed over; he threw her body away from him, stood and clamped his head between his hands, and roared in pain. Something was in his way, restraining him; he thrashed against it, and it shattered. The room was on fire, but it didn't seem to matter; he kicked and thrashed his way to the window and threw himself through it.

It seemed like every bit of pleasure he had ever drawn from warp spells was demanding its price in pain twice over and all at once. He waited for the impact with the ground to smash him straight into the void, but instead he caught himself on wings he did not remember summoning. He climbed into the storm at a muscle burning pace, screaming in pain as he did so.

Impossibly, the pain was still building. He had long since been certain that it could not get any worse, and yet it continued to build, and he had to get away from it. He saw the nexus of the warp storm below him, and he turned to dive into it, and he remembered one forbidden spell outcome that he had known better than to investigate for a hidden warp spell; it was too obviously simply fatal. Even as the pain continued to build in his body, he cleared his mind of any concept of location and twisted his thoughts into the patterns of a teleport spell. He hit the energy ball at the center of the warpstorm, and teleported to nowhere.

Kelestor returned to consciousness and little else. He had no awareness of his body, and all of his senses were disturbingly quiet. He wondered if this were the void, and wondered how long it would take his consciousness to disintegrate. Of course, since he wasn't inclined to boredom, he attempted to entertain himself as best he could, with only the contents of his own mind to work with. His life had not been long, but it had been fairly full, and he had read a great many books.

He soon realized that there was no satisfaction in anything that lacked a strong narrative, but his memory held several novels, a few biographies, and of course his own life. It disturbed him that when he laid the narratives side by side, he liked his own story least. He had unquestionably been a villain, and a rather lackluster villain at that. He would have to do something about that if he ever got out of this whatever it was.

It was not completely silent; there were occasional sounds dimly heard, and other odd flashes of sensation, but they seldom lasted for very long, and he could not make sense of them. He did find, however, that three new stories were being added to his collection. One of them was yet another retelling of the war between Elethay and Jikadell. It bothered him that his sympathies were with Elethay, and yet he had lived under Jikadell's banner.

Another of the new tales was the story of Valaria the heretic, and the third was the story of an amnesiac orc whose moral resolve was absolutely terrifying. Kelestor admired him, and fervently hoped he would never meet him. He was fairly certain he could kill the orc, if it came to that, but he was also fairly certain it WOULD come to that, and that would be a shame.

There were voices in the distance again, and as always Kelestor concentrated on them; this time he found he could actually hear what was being said.

"Because we NEED a doorway; it's in the nature of the exercise," said a cultured male voice.

"And the universe will conform itself to our needs?" asked a gruff male voice.

"Not the universe, no," said the cultured voice. "Just this odd little piece of it. And I suspect that things would go easier if you would relax and believe in it."

"You want him to believe in what he sees?" asked a female voice. "When he knows that it isn't real?"

"You're not helping," said the cultured voice. "Do you want this to turn into a discussion of metaphysics? For us, at this moment, what we see is absolutely real. It's just a little more malleable than the world he's used to."

Kelestor found that if he focused on a single speaker, he could get a sense of the person. Though they all seemed to be humanoid, the cultured voice was a dragon; the woman was a unicorn. The gruff voice… the owner of the gruff voice had avoided classification, somehow. Kelestor wondered what that meant.

"Here, you see?" said the dragon. "A doorway. And behind it… Fascinating metaphor, Quill. This should be interesting."

"Excuse me?" asked the gruff voice, as Kelestor realized that this might be the orc from his story.

"We are in a labyrinth lined with books. It must be a metaphor for the way you see your own mind," said the dragon.

"Do you have any idea how Ravin died?" asked the unicorn. "I'm beginning to think someone may have stabbed him to shut him up."

The dragon laughed, and the gruff voice answered, "We could ask him, but then we would have to listen to the answer." There was more laughter.

"I thought we were going to run into nightmare creatures," said the gruff voice.

"Do you have nightmares?" asked the dragon. "We are trying to find the girl, and set her free. Anything else we run into is just your own mental clutter, and there seems to be precious little of that. Probably the result of your memory loss."

The girl? Kelestor wondered about that. If they were looking for the unicorn girl he had killed, then they were probably also looking for him, and they were enemies. He did his best to focus more closely on the intruders.

There was something about the dragon and the unicorn... Kelestor realized that there was a spell of some kind supporting their presence. The third person— the orc— Quill— was different. He belonged in a way that the other two didn't. And it was definitely preferable to deal with one enemy rather than three. Kelestor concentrated on the dragon, attempted a simple counterspell, and the dragon disappeared. Kelestor would have smiled if he had had a face to smile with.

"What happened to Ravin?" the unicorn asked; there was a touch of panic in her voice that Kelestor enjoyed.

"He was thrown out. I imagine you're next. Thanks for trying," Quill answered her calmly. Kelestor attempted to grind teeth that didn't exist and prepared a second counterspell.

"Good luck, Quill. I'm sorry I wasn't more help," said the unicorn. She threw her arms around Quill and kissed him energetically, then disappeared as the dispel hit her. The exchange made Kelestor angry for some reason.

Quill continued down the dark, book lined corridor; Kelestor continued to watch and found that he hated him. This pathetic orc had started with nothing and had made himself a hero's reputation and a circle of loyal friends in a few short months; Kelestor had, or had once had, power and money and a circle of sycophants, but never admiration. Kelestor would kill him.

Quill's corridor came to an end, and now he was in the room where Kelestor had killed the unicorn girl. The girl was lying right where she had fallen, and there was a book that Kelestor did not recognize on the table. Quill healed the girl's throat; she revived and he wrapped her in a blanket and helped her to her feet.

"Quill?" the girl said uncertainly. "What happened to Lord Sar? Was it all a dream?"

Quill shook his head. "No, I don't think it was a dream. More likely this is a dream; I would have thought the wound on your throat was fatal. I take it you are Tayma?"

The girl nodded. "I am Athame Sweetwater, though everyone calls me Tayma. What happened to Lord Sar?"

"Again that name. And who is Lord Sar, Tayma?" Quill asked.

"Kelestor Sar is a guest of my master's; I was assigned to him. He is said to be a great scholar of Necromancy."

"Wonderful," Quill said disgustedly. He picked up the alien volume. "This has his name on it; let's see what it has to say. Have a seat; this may be a while." Quill sat at the table, opened the book, and began to read.

As soon as Quill opened the book, Kelestor's ability to see Quill and his surroundings began to fade, and in moments the room was lost to Kelestor's sight. He found that he once again had a body, and that he was in the same book lined corridor in which he had watched Quill. He shrugged, guessed at which direction he had to go, and set off.

Eventually the corridor ended at a blank panel; Kelestor pushed on it, and it opened into a small room with a large doorway at the far end. The panel Kelestor had pushed turned out to be the back of another bookshelf, and the door from the doorway opposite had been torn off of its hinges. Through the door was a large, high-ceilinged room lined with books, and in the far side of that was another door.

Kelestor sensed that the world of the living was beyond that door; he ran to it, opened it, and stepped through blindly. The world wrenched, and suddenly he was lying on his back in a darkened room. He heard an unknown voice say, "Perrin! He's shifting!"

A powerful hand clamped on Kelestor's throat; a bass voice said, "Hold him down; don't let him up, and try to stop him from doing magic." Kelestor fought to control himself and choke back the panic. If he could just get off a couple of spells, buy himself some breathing room, and then teleport away…

Kelestor was pulled violently back into the large, high-ceilinged room. He tumbled like a rag doll, then looked up to see Quill standing over him. "It's not that easy, Lord Sar. It's not going to be NEARLY that easy," Quill growled.

Kelestor rose to his feet carefully; he saw the girl (now fully clothed, a fact which irritated Kelestor far more than it should have) standing behind Quill. "You're ME," Kelestor answered; he tried to make it sound accusatory, but it was mostly incredulous.

Quill responded with a slow blink. "If you wish," he said quietly. "Have you solved the whole riddle yet, Kelestor? What happened that night? Why does

Tayma still exist? For that matter, why do I exist at all?"

Kelestor looked at Tayma briefly, then back at Quill. "Something aborted the Death Drain..."

"Something that caused you, or made the aborted spell cause you, intense pain." Quill advanced slowly as he spoke, driving Kelestor back into the alcove with the ruined door. "So instead of consuming Tayma's soul, you welded it to your own. She's trapped here, a mind with no body and only enough soul to sustain it. Makes you proud, doesn't it?"

Kelestor's back was to the wall now; he tried to find the hidden door, but it seemed to be gone, and he was afraid to take his eyes off of Quill. "I needed to know what it felt like, and she was doomed anyway..."

"By the Lady, you disgust me. Did you ever do ANYTHING worthwhile when you weren't reading?" Quill spat out the words; he was only a short reach from Kelestor now.

Kelestor looked up suddenly. "I had wings," he said. "Why did I have wings that night?"

Quill smiled coldly, "I don't know, Kelestor, why did you have wings that night?"

Kelestor thought back; there was something... he looked behind Quill to the girl. "You!" he said. "You saw something, just before you died. Tell me what it was."

Tayma walked around Quill until she could see both of their faces. She looked at Quill and he shrugged. "Tell him if you want. He has no power here," Quill said.

Tayma nodded and sighed. "You turned into a dragon," she said quietly.

Telestor's eyes widened. "Yes! I remember now… But you were already there. You wouldn't let me hit the ground."

"Something like that," Quill said quietly. "Not really, but something like that."

"But why did it hurt so much? I never knew there could be that much pain…"

Quill shrugged. "I don't know. It may not have been real. It may have been the aborted spell; it may have been my consciousness emerging. It may just have been your conscience. You don't strike me as the type to handle pain well."

"But… What do we do now? We have three minds and two souls in a single body; I've never heard of such a thing." Kelestor's curiosity began to take the edge off of his fear and confusion.

"We?" Quill growled. "We don't do anything. There is no 'we'. YOU finish the job you started, and flutter off to the Void, and leave me to live my life."

"But… No. I am a master necromancer. You're a common warrior," Kelestor said as he finally began to find his sense of self. "I'll destroy you. I'll…"

"How? If you destroy me, you destroy yourself. The only way to be rid of me is to get me to concede, and go voluntarily. Which will never happen." Quill grinned wickedly as he spoke. "You aren't tough enough to live as a dragon in this world, Kelestor. Particularly as a dragon who is also a former necromancer who has no friends. And even more particularly, as a person who has a personal torturer living in his head making every conscious moment as miserable as possible." Quill punctuated his words by backhanding Kelestor in the face; Kelestor fell full length to the floor.

"Leave, Kelestor. Give up. Quit. I am perfectly willing to destroy myself to take you out of the world, and you don't have the stomach for the fight. You really don't."

Kelestor looked up at Tayma. "What about her?"

"You killed her, monster. Do you think she wants to continue existing trapped in YOUR head?" Quill kicked him in the face. "Leave, Kelestor. It's over."

Kelestor looked up with bleary eyes and saw one of Quill's eyes starting to swell shut. "When you hit me… You feel it," he said incredulously. Quill nodded, shrugged, and stamped on one of Kelestor's hands; Kelestor bounced away from the pain and whimpered, "You're insane."

Quill smiled through the bruises. "No, just determined. Leave."

Kelestor's face lit up. "I'll kill the girl."

Quill looked at him, thought for a moment, then calmly bent back one of his own fingers until it broke. Kelestor doubled up in pain. "I can't stop you," he said quietly. "I've already decided that your death is worth her life. Now we're just playing out the endgame." He broke another finger.

"Do you want a happy thought to take to the void with you, Kelestor?" Quill asked, as he backhanded the wall with his maimed hand. "You were well educated, and you had excellent taste in literature." He broke another finger. "That, it seems, is what you built me out of. The rest was just a complete waste." He used his good hand to ball the maimed one into a fist, a process which brought gasps of pain from Kelestor. "For those things, I will always be grateful to you. Now GO!" he roared, and slammed the maimed fist into the wall with all of his strength.

Kelestor screamed and writhed, then was still. He turned to look at Quill. "Gratitude, at least, for that," he said quietly.

Quill nodded. "At least for that." Kelestor nodded once, and faded away.

Quill leaned against the wall and slumped to the floor; Tayma rushed to his side. "Is there anything I can do?" she asked.

Quill looked at her with his broken face and grinned. "You? Are asking me?" He shook his head and moaned at the sensation. "Let me catch my breath, and do a bit of healing magic, and I will be fine." Tayma nodded and waited. Quill did nothing for a long while, and then used witchcraft to repair his hand and his face. When he was done he looked at Tayma and said quietly, "What do YOU want?"

Tayma spread her hands in bewilderment. "What is there? I'm dead."

Quill nodded. "There is that. But you're also bonded to me, somehow, and I'm not dead. So you can either stay with me, and share as much of my life as you are able, or I can arrange to have you sent to the Void. Neither one of them strikes me as particularly desirable."

Tayma smiled. "You don't mind if I stay?"

Quill shook his head. "You are welcome to haunt me in any manner you wish, for as long as you wish. I just wish I had more to offer you."

Tayma smiled more broadly. "Then I will stay." She hugged him, and he winced.

Quill got to his feet. "I think it is time to rejoin the others," he said. He took

Tayma's hand, and walked through the door to the outer world.

Fourteen: Departures

The most crippling limits are those set upon us by our detractors, and we are
ever our own greatest detractors. There are limits everywhere, but WHERE?
How do we know a thing is impossible until we have attempted it, and failed?
And even then, how do we know that if we had only done things a tiny bit
differently, we might have succeeded? To be truly alive is to be constantly
hurling ourselves at the barriers which our perception has placed before us,
and the only way to truly know if a barrier is real or not is to break it.

—Xart Oglevert, "Cyclopedia of Aerodynamics and Aerobatics"

There was an iron clamp across my face that was riveted to my skull and jaw;
it was impossible to speak, and difficult to breathe. I heard Perrin's voice
say, "It's all right; you can let him up, 'Bacco." The clamp resolved itself into
Bacco's hand as he took it away, and I drew a deep breath.

There were more people in the room than there should have been; Perrin and
Jasmine and Chalice-Leaf were there from the start, and I knew that 'Bacco
had been right outside the door in case of trouble. But the others... I suddenly
realized that the others were all at least mildly translucent, and then I began
to recognize them: Ravin, Chalice-Storm, Tayma, and a gray-bearded dwarf
whom I did not know, but who looked vaguely like Perrin. All of the ghosts,
and Perrin, were busy interrogating Tayma, who seemed overwhelmed. I sat
up and cleared my throat loudly. All eyes turned to me.

"I'm home," I said. "Doesn't anyone want to know what happened?" All but Tayma and 'Bacco started to bombard me with questions; Tayma shrank against the wall looking grateful, and 'Bacco just grinned his usual wicked grin. I considered trying to sort out the cacophony, but decided against it and just gave them some time to run down.

"'Bacco," I finally asked, "Can you see him, or him, or her, or her?" I indicated the ghosts. "'Bacco glared at me and shook his head. I nodded. "Perrin, why can I see disembodied ghosts?"

Perrin and the gray dwarf looked at each other; the gray dwarf spoke. "Tell him he seems to be starting down the shaman's path, in which case this young lady would seem to be his spirit guide."

Perrin opened his mouth, but I waved him off. "I can hear you as well, Grandfather. But I don't believe we've been introduced."

The old dwarf smiled and offered me a spectral hand. "Meligrant Stonebow." He indicated Perrin. "The young tyrant's great-grandfather." I nodded, and took and shook the proffered hand as well as I could; I could feel it, but it had no substance.

I looked at all of them. "Is there anyone here who thinks they have a better idea of what just happened than I do?" Heads shook and negative grunts were made; I nodded. "Then here is my version of it, guesses and all." I indicated Jasmine, Autumn, and 'Bacco. "You three. Just so you have some idea of what's going on, I can see four ghosts in the room: Ravin, Stormchaser, Perrin's great-grandfather Meligrant, and Athame Sweetwater, usually known as Tayma. She had the bad luck to change into a unicorn for the first time directly in front of a rather nasty Necromancer, which is why she's dead."

I took a deep breath and continued. "Once upon a time there was an Ebonese wizard named Kelestor Sar. He was a thaumatologist, a magical theoretician, and he taught himself necromancy, and he became addicted to casting warp spells. Before too long he had to leave the Celestial Kingdom, and he went north into Haskalad territory.

"The Haskalads loved him. He seemed to know every warp spell that had ever been conceived, and he was willing to teach them in exchange for fairly modest considerations, so he quickly became very rich, even if he wasn't very powerful politically. But even though he knew all sorts of warp magic, he had never done a single drain spell, because he had never had access to a shapeshifter. It seems that under Haskalad law you have to be a pretty high noble to be allowed to use necromancy. They made a loophole for Kelestor as long as he was a useful teacher, but he still wasn't a Blazeblood, and they would have killed him if he had tried to steal one of their shapeshifters.

"And then one night, he had a sex slave in his room, and a warp storm passed over, and the girl changed into a unicorn right in front of him, and he realized that he could drain her, and no one would notice the warp because there was already a storm overhead, and he could make up some excuse for killing the girl because she was just a slave.

"So he did it, and in the process caught an enormous dose of the Storm Seeding, and turned into a dragon himself. And the girl... It's a weak metaphor, but the girl got stuck in his metaphysical throat. He couldn't consume her, and he couldn't get rid of her. And then there was the fact that he was much older than most first time shifters, and that he was just FULL of residual warp energy from all of the spells he had cast...

"He lost his mind, I guess. He was in hideous pain, and he realized that the life he had built for himself was OVER, and somehow... He reached back into his memories to the heroic stories he had loved when he was a small boy, and he built or summoned or FOUND someone who could deal with the pain and all of the complications and survive. And then he flew straight into the nexus of the warp storm and did a blind teleport."

Perrin got it. He had spent at least as much time working on the riddle as I had. "And the next morning you woke up in a meadow several hundred miles away. Interesting. Can't say I've ever heard of anything like that happening before. So what became of the necromancer?"

I shook my head. "My best guess is that he was unconscious until tonight; he was dreaming of what I was doing, sometimes. But the spell we used tonight seems to have brought him to full consciousness. He managed to dispel the connections that gave Ravin and Stormchaser the ability to function inside my mind, but Tayma and I really lived there, and he had to take another approach.

"It came down to a contest of will, and Kelestor didn't have a chance. He was a warp junkie, and I, Goddess help me, am a storybook hero."

Autumnleaf chuckled. "We already knew THAT, Quill. We just didn't know that the storybook had already been written." She was smiling; Perrin was deep in thought; Jasmine and 'Bacco still looked puzzled. The ghosts were deep in conversation with one another.

I looked around the room and saw Brindle on a high shelf, staring intently at me. I stared back, and found myself saying, "Hello, Cat. What do you think of all of this foolishness?" Except that I didn't say it, I just threw the thoughts at her. Brindle reacted as if I had slapped her, then returned to her original pose and cocked her head to the side. I had a strange sensation that she was getting closer and closer to me, though she didn't actually move.

"Quill?" said an unfamiliar voice in my mind. "How did you do that?"

"Brindle?" I answered; I was as surprised as she was. "I'm not sure; let me think about it."

"You can hear me? I can talk to you? This is WONDERFUL!" Brindle launched herself across the room and caromed and bounced her way into my lap. She looked up at me, and again I could hear her voice. "So when do I get to go flying again, huh?"

I laughed at that. "Soon, silly Cat. Very soon." I looked around the room again; no one was paying much attention. I stood and took off my clothes, then reached inside myself and…

If you have never shifted shape, it is hard to describe the sensations accurately. It should hurt; your skin is stretching in some places and shrinking in others; your bones are dancing and reshaping themselves under your skin, and you joints are pretty much all dislocated. It should hurt a great deal, but it doesn't. It actually feels good, in a sun-on-your-face, scent-of-fresh-baked-bread sort of way. I looked around the room again through unaccustomed eyes and saw that everyone was watching me.

"I TOLD you he was a dragon," came Ravin's smug voice. "Interesting that he chose the miniature form, though. And I have NEVER seen that color on a dragon before."

"He looks like a dragon storm," Autumnleaf said softly.

"He looks like a Soul Gem," growled Perrin. "Like a polished piece of Taintstone."

I squatted back on my haunches and looked at my front claws; my scales were a purple so deep it seemed black except when the light hit it, and they were streaked with veins of red and blue."

"Quill!" Brindle's voice sounded in my head. "You've got wings! No fair!" I turned to glare at Brindle, realized there was no draconic equivalent to licking my lips hungrily (too many sharp teeth) and settled for ducking my head at Brindle and snapping my jaws. She jumped backward and rolled under a piece of furniture.

I turned to Perrin. "Any other questions?" I thought at him, and he flinched a bit as he heard me.

"Mindspeech, too," Perrin said. "Not bad for a first try. No, go try out your wings if you want. Just stay low, and keep back from the river." I nodded and went out the door with Brindle behind me.

"You heard what Perrin said, Cat. Stay low, and to the west. Can you live with that?" I sent to Brindle; she nodded and I cast the Wizard Wings spell. Brindle charged into the air with a cry of "Can't catch me!" and I set out to prove her wrong.

Brindle was as fast as I was, and more maneuverable, but she had no skill at all and telegraphed her maneuvers, even in the darkness. I could easily have snatched her out of the air with my jaws, or shredded her wings with my claws, but that wasn't my purpose. I wanted to fly, and to let her fly. I could hear her giggling happily in my mind. I let her tire herself out, and then herded her back to Ferrypoint before the spell expired and left her wingless.

I found Perrin waiting with my clothing; the others had gone off to bed, and there were no ghosts in evidence. I returned to my accustomed form and got dressed; Perrin played with his pipe and scratched Brindle's head.

"There is just nothing simple about you, is there, Quill?" Perrin said at last. I didn't respond. "Spirit speakers are trained to set limits on spirits before they are allowed to bond with a guide. The ones who don't usually end up being consumed by the spirits. And now you've bonded with this girl, and gone out of your way to set no limits on her at all. Not to mention that there are all sorts of stories about why it is a bad idea to have a spirit guide who is of the opposite sex." He smiled slightly and shook his head.

Brindle looked up at him quizzically; she asked me, "What is he talking about?"

"I don't know, Cat," I said aloud. "I think he is talking about Tayma."

Brindle looked at me suspiciously. "Who's Tayma?"

"A dead unicorn who lives inside my head, I guess. We're still trying to sort that out."

Brindle scowled at me, then hissed as Perrin lifted her by the scruff of the neck and looked into her eyes. "'Bacco's right," he said sourly. "You really do manage to find an odd way to do everything. NO ONE acquires a Spirit Guide and a familiar on the same evening." I bowed my head and clenched my teeth; Brindle demonstrated a surprising mastery of profanity, of which Perrin was mercifully unaware. "There isn't time to help you through this, Quill. You'll have to get those Haskalads, and the rest of your menagerie, out of here long before I can teach you anything useful for dealing with this. So you might as well go as soon as possible, and try to find help fast once you are across the ridge. Are you up to a march tomorrow?"

"I think so," I answered.

Perrin nodded. "The one thing that saves you in all of this is that the girl is so TINY," Perrin continued. "If she weren't... Well, WELDED is as good a word as any, I guess... to you, she wouldn't have survived at all; she would have gone straight off to the void. And you're so much tougher than that it's almost a joke. Just make sure you stay in control."

"I intend to," I answered.

"Then get some rest. See you in the morning." Perrin clamped his pipe between his teeth and stalked off.

We did set out the next morning, but we didn't actually leave Ferrypoint for good for several days. We made a trek to Whisky's campsite at the foot of Blackwater, and left the three Haskalads there in the care of Willow, Stragus, and Ghost. Whisky and I returned to Ferrypoint, then made two more trips to the camp with pack horses, stocking the camp with supplies; we would leave with heavy packs.

During the time in Ferrypoint between trips, Perrin pronounced me a journeyman blacksmith, saying that there was bound to be someone worse than me somewhere who was making a living at it. Perrin also spent three full days teaching Chalice, Philo, and me how to construct mind to mind channel links. He said that having a dragon (me) who could blast through the initial resistance made the teaching process much easier.

I know that I was getting much more used to having voices in my head that weren't mine than I ever would have expected. I was AWARE of Brindle even when she wasn't talking to me, and she talked to me more that I really appreciated. And then there was Tayma, of whom I was very seldom aware except when I was asleep, and then she made it very clear that she had been watching everything I did all day long, and she always had several hundred questions. After a few days she learned to talk to me when I was conscious, and a few days after that she learned how to talk to Brindle.

The ability to see unmanifested ghosts that I had had at the end of the spiritwalk was temporary, though I could still see Tayma whenever she chose to wander outside of her sanctuary in my head. When I worked in the smithy with Perrin, Tayma often had conversations with Meligrant; I could hear and see only Tayma's side of things, and I learned from Perring that he could only hear and see Meligrant's side unless he cast a Spirit Vision spell to see it all. It surprised me that Brindle could see Tayma as well, though Perrin told me that was normal when a person had both a familiar and a spirit guide.

For the most part, Tayma took up residence in my dreams, and from there we explored our memories together. I had only a few months of memories that were truly mine; Tayma had nearly twenty years to call her own, and Kelestor's dismal swamp covered most of fifty years. We became good friends, though she never really overcame the subservience that a lifetime of slavery had beaten into her; perhaps that was just as well, given Perrin's dire warnings about spirits that were too powerful.

I finally got a chance to ask Perrin about that warning as we were loading the horses for our final departure from Ferrypoint, and he just rolled his eyes. "If you get along well, you tend to want to spend your entire life inside of your head," he said with a grin. "Though I doubt you'll be able to get away with that."

I nodded; "I can see both sides of that already," I said. "And if we don't get along?"

Perrin's grin turned a bit nasty. "Then there is no place to hide." He shook his head, and the warmth was back in his smile. "You'll do fine, Quill. There's nothing ahead of you worse than what you've already been through."

We left at the first light of the false dawn; Whisky led, followed by Philo leading one of the horses, then Chalice (with Pepper at her side) leading the other horse (with Brindle enthroned in the luggage) and I brought up the rear. Perrin, Jasmine, 'Bacco, and a small assortment of vermites saw us off.

We took two days longer getting to the rendezvous than a direct route required; I asked Whisky to lead us on a detour to the north. It was mid-morning on the third day out of Ferrypoint when Whisky called a halt in a large meadow.

"Quill?" he called back. "This is it." I walked to where he was standing, and he pointed out a small tree that had been gnawed off near its base.

"Yes," I answered. "This is it." I pulled the sword I had chosen for this occasion out of one of the horse packs and walked to the center of the meadow; it was a nondescript sword that had belonged to one of the men in the caravan I had killed. I turned around until I felt sure I was in the center of the meadow, then drove the sword point first into the ground until the quillons touched the earth. That done, I rejoined the others.

"Quill?" Chalice asked. "What was that about?"

"The stump will have rotted away in a few years," I replied. "The sword should last a hundred. I just wanted to make sure I could find this place again, if I ever wanted to."

Chalice still didn't understand, but Pepper did. She had seen me use the spear I had gnawed from that stump, and was holding a walking stick that had been carved from that spear. "Chalice," she said quietly, "He was born here."

Appendix One: Leaving Grandilar

I had plans for more of *Storybook Orc*; I had a vague outline of a full novel, and detailed outlines of the next several chapters. Brindle was going to turn out to be a Tigrean, and Pepper and Tayma were going to form a partnership, becoming a Vermite-Elf-Unicorn. Quill was going to adopt a dead horse as a familiar. But the writing process stalled after I finished chapter 14.

There were problems with writing in someone else's world, and they got worse as time went on. Black Dragon (*Dragon Storm*'s publisher) was managing the world with game marketing as a primary concern, and this conflicted significantly with my desires. I went through several cycles of getting drawn back in, and becoming very active in the game, and then getting frustrated and walking away again. Eventually I walked away and never went back; there were things going on in the world that made it hard for me to believe in it, and I didn't have the authority to fix them.

As much as I love this story, and this world, and these characters, I decided that it was foolish of me to invest my infrequent creative impulses into something over which I had so little control. But it was hardly a total loss; some of the ideas and characters that started here migrated into my other work. Perrin has contributed epigraphs to my novel *Fiddler's Rose*; flight wizard Xart and his writings have turned up in two additional worlds, and a dagger made from the horn of a unicorn, to which the ghost of a unicorn is bound, is central to *Fiddler's Rose*.

There follow a few other fragments of my excursion into Grandilar. Appendix Two contains an essay on the three main schools of magic, which represents my most successful effort to modify the shape of the world; it was written after a great deal of back and forth with world designer Susan Van Camp, and was eventually published on the Black Dragon website. Its main inspiration was a rumor that came to me about characters who were both Witches and Necromancers, an idea that seemed very wrong for the world.

Appendix Three is my version of an orc creation myth that I gleaned from personal correspondence with Susan. It was never official, but it fits into the world as it was at that time, and I think it is kind of amusing.

Appendix Four is a scene that would have been in the first chapter or two of the next section of *Storybook Orc*, and it deals with Quill befriending an undead horse. Given that the undead are pretty much invariably evil in Dragon Storm, this idea was met by the player community with everything from disgust to outrage, with a couple of more savvy people being merely curious. The thing is, skeletons and zombies are invariably evil, but ghosts can be anything. And I have always been fascinated by the idea of lonely ghosts bound into their own remains. I find this scene beautiful and kind of heart-breaking, and an excellent note on which to step away from the world.

Appendix Two: Three Schools of Magic

Be it known that on the tenth day of the second month of the third year of his reign, His Royal Highness King Lenarius of Selenay expressed a desire to learn to practice magic, and tasked me with determining which of the various schools of magic would be best suited for the study of a king. My report follows.

First, it is well known that there are three schools of magic each with different philosophies and methods for gathering supernatural energy—Od—and harnessing it to effect the natural world. One Master I questioned, a practitioner of all three disciplines, spoke of the three philosophies in terms of the ways a person might gather water. "The Witch," he told me, "Draws Od from the richness of Elethay, much as a man might draw water from a river. The water is abundant, but the river goes where it will, and the man must follow it. The Shaman draws his water from a rain barrel. He may build his house where he pleases, and while there is water in the barrel it is easy to get, but his supply is always dependent on the whims of the rain. The Wizard draws his water from a well he has dug himself; he will have water when he wants it, where he wants it, but it will always be work to draw it up from the depths of the earth."

My king, I was very confused by this at first (though Your Highness will no doubt understand it at once), but over time I realized that it illustrates some very basic truths of the three schools.

Witchcraft

Witchcraft draws its energy from the physical plane, and is in many ways the least demanding of the crafts. But it should be noted that Witchcraft is inextricably linked to the worship of Elethay (not a bad thing, for a devout man like Your Highness); most Elethay clergy are witches, and any witch can act as clergy if the need arises. The mechanism which witches use to tap the Od of nature and harness it is one of harmony and conformity with the earth, and the goddess. The witch must be aware of, and consonant with, the "web of nature" at all times, and witches who deliberately act in disregard of the "Heart of the Goddess" will soon find their powers failing. I have heard it said that one does not learn witchcraft; one attunes oneself to the Goddess, and the spells follow naturally.

Since all witches have the Goddess in common, it is unheard of for any two witches to be enemies in their own persons. Two witches may dislike each other, but they will still respect each other; two witches may face each other across a battlefield, but they will always work for peace between two nations which both acknowledge Elethay. Witches will also always have an affinity for animals, which does not so much mean that all animals will like all witches (though many witches do have an uncanny ability to relate to animals), but that all witches will respect all animals, even if they find them hostile or terrifying. It is said that the true daughter of Elethay sees the beauty of the wild beasts even as they devour her.

Shamanism

Shamanism draws on the Spirit plane as its source of Od; this requires shamans to develop a high degree of sensitivity to spirits and the Spirit Plane, which usually interferes with their ability to deal with the natural world somewhat. Shamans tend to seem distracted and out of focus; this is because they are seeing a broader world than those who do not follow the shaman's path. The "rain" of the old master's analogy represents the fact that when the shaman reaches for Od on the Spirit Plane, he gets NOTHING unless he has a spirit in that plane to direct it into his hand. All shamans have at least one Spirit Guide; many have several. Spirit Guides can range in power from weak spirits who can only manifest in the shaman's own dreams to spirits so powerful they can manifest for days at a time (though such are very rare). Shamans generally have much more freedom of action and attitude than do witches; a strong shaman with a weak Spirit Guide can bully his guide to do whatever he wishes; a clever shaman will find a Spirit Guide who shares his own attitudes and goals. Of course, it is not unknown for powerful Spirit Guides to reduce their respective shamans to servants or even slaves; the shaman's path is horribly dangerous for the careless or the unprepared.

Shamans have certain characteristics in common, but this does not include any kind of moral direction. A shaman who is guided by dead ancestors (as, in fact, most shamans are) will be loyal to the goals of his family; a shaman who is guided by spirits of evil will himself be evil. Shamans who have not been called to their task by specific spirits (usually ancestors) will usually attempt to locate spirit guides who will agree with their goals and follow their wishes, whatever those might be.

Wizardry

Wizardry looks to the astral plane for Od, and the only thing that shapes the magic is the wizard's will. There is neither divine assistance nor spirit guidance involved. Thus, while wizardry requires the greatest amount of effort, it also offers the greatest amount of freedom. The are currently two subclasses of wizards practicing in Selenay; one group calls itself the Prismatic School, and every wizard I spoke to was a follower of this tradition. The other group is known as the Collegium Obscurum, and what little I know of it is from wizards who have left it and joined the Prismatic School.

Wizardry accomplishes magical effects by channeling Od through a mind in which certain specific patterns of thought exist. Prismatic wizards create these patterns by visualizing light of different colors passing through various lenses of different colors to produce a specific pattern of shapes and colors on a three dimensional surface. A wizard showed me a device which contained four light sources and eight lenses, all of which could be moved, and told me that a student needed to be able to visualize this device in all of its permutations before he could cast a spell. (No wonder wizards keep such elaborate notebooks!) I have been told that other colleges have used different tools; certainly a college once existed that used music rather than light as its focus, as did another which used only complex shapes, and a third which used only abstract symbols, but none of these currently exist in Selenay.

Prismatic wizards study for a very long time before they can cast a single spell, but once they reach that point, it is relatively easy to learn new spells, and even to improvise spells that one has seen but never studied. It is still a very difficult thing to develop a spell which has never before existed, however. The Obscurantists follow a different path; they teach each spell as a separate entity, without bothering with the central knowledge from which the spell flows. Thus, their apprentices cast their first spells early in their training, but never acquire the ability to learn new spells quickly that is characteristic of the Prismatic School. Obscurantists seem to like things this way; they lure their students with easy power, but keep them on a short leash. Given that the Obscurantists are rumored to be experimenting with Warp magics (warp is known to most wizards as a toxic side effect of mis-cast spells) and even with Necromancy, this is hardly surprising.

All that can be said of wizards as a group is that they are intelligent, patient, and make very bad enemies; beyond that, they are as varied as humans (and humanoids) in general.

Conclusion

Such is my report, your Highness. My conclusion is simple: A King must be his own man, and of the three magicians, only the wizard is master of his own course. I must say that even wizardry requires a long apprenticeship, and I can only wonder if it is appropriate for a monarch to subject himself to a master, even on a temporary basis. But I am not a monarch, and my judgement of such things is no doubt faulty.

Dennold of Bridgeport, Scribe to His Majesty

Gaming notes:

This is intended to give information to players who want to know their characters a little better. None of it is intended to have any direct effect on game mechanics. In a nutshell:

Witches are naturally religious people. They are in tune with nature, and they hate warp with a passion. Also, as noted above, they tend to respect and trust other witches, even if they don't LIKE them. Witches will be VERY inclined to have familiars, and pets.

Shamans are always going to be a bit spirit addled when nothing else is going on. And, as it says, they will always have at least one Spirit Guide. Unless/until more appropriate cards are released, Spirit Guides can be assumed to be ancestor spirits who are just powerful enough to make themselves heard by the shaman whenever they want. They can't manifest physically in any way, though the gamemaster may rule that a Warding spirit is the Spirit Guide. Spirit Guides are intended to be role-play aids for the gamemaster to use, abuse, or ignore as he wishes. Spirit Guides of Spirit Speakers will almost certainly be ancestors of the character; Spirit Guides of characters who earn the Shaman card can be anything that makes sense, including dead player characters.

Wizards is wizards. You were expecting something else? Wizards on Grandilar are similar in outlook and temperament to wizards in most other games. One interesting point: While wizards are trained to improvise spells off the central body of prismatic spell craft, warp magic does NOT flow out of that body of knowledge. Just another reason why player wizards don't use warp magic.

Appendix Three: Orc Creation Myth

There follows a story that Orc Shamans only tell to their most trusted apprentices, or to strangers when they have had much too much warped squirrel jerky:

"Long and long ago, after the great storms that only the dragons survived, the dragons had no one to serve them, for there were no mortals. And it happened that at that time there was a she-dragon who was such a mighty warrior that she did exactly as she pleased, and ignored the elders of her clan. And at the same time there was a he-dragon who was such a learned magician that none of the others could understand him. And the other dragons resented these two, and were jealous of them. And one day the other dragons got together and said, "We should craft a mighty ritual, and take these two who think they are better than us, and make them into servants." And so they did, and they bound the she-dragon warrior and the he-dragon wizard into new shapes that were small enough that no dragon need ever fear them, but yet strong and hardy and dexterous enough to be effective servants. And the two became Grandmother and Grandfather Orc, and from them all orcs are descended."

If you have the temerity to ask an elder dragon about this story, she is likely to be mortally offended, but if she chooses to comment at all, she will tell you that the she-dragon was actually a notorious brigand, and that the he-dragon was actually a drooling lunatic, and that the story isn't true anyway.

The truth is that no one knows, but there must be some reason that even though orcs have as much dragon's blood as any other of the mortal races, they don't produce shape shifters.

Appendix Four: The Necormancer's Horse

The final loose end was the necromancer's horse, which had been quietly and deliberately smashing his former master into paste with its left fore hoof while we were treating our wounded. I had deliberately positioned myself so that I could watch it while Chalice did her embroidery on my various wounds.

It was an amazing thing, really, as much a work of mundane craft as of magic. Its long bones had been plated in bronze, and its joints replaced with heavy bronze hinges; its face was a bronze mask with a decidedly draconic caste, and its eyes glowed red with magical fire captured in crystal. The saddle seemed to be built into the creature's back, and there seemed to be some kind of container inside its ribcage. A necromancer had brought the horse back to life, but some metalsmith had put a great deal of time, effort, and craft into making it what it was. I wondered which influence was stronger.

When Chalice had finished her ministrations, I rose and walked to within a few paces of the horse; those burning red eyes turned to focus on me, and I noticed with interest that the faceplate allowed the horse to look straight ahead with both eyes, predator style. I dug through my cranial detritus for the ability to speak mind to mind that I knew was there, even though I was still extremely inexperienced at it. I activated the spell.

"Greetings, brother horse," I said. "I am called Quill."

"I have several names," the horse replied, "And I like none of them."

"That seems to me a sad thing," I offered.

"It does not make me happy," the horse said. "But it has never seemed that my happiness was anyone's concern."

I nodded. "I need to deal with you, somehow. I can not just set you free; you will be hunted down, and either destroyed or enslaved by another necromancer. Or I could free your spirit to the Void."

The horse's head drooped. "I do not like those options."

"What do you WANT, then?"

The horse's head came up, and those deliberately hellish eyes looked into mine. "There are four things that are thought to be of great value to my people: To eat well, to mate and raise progeny; to feel the warmth of the sun on your skin; to run freely." The horse raised its head and looked around for a moment, then continued. "I no longer eat; I am gelded. I have no skin, but I still feel the sun, and I can run as no horse has ever run before. I would keep what I have."

I smiled; I could work with that. "That may be possible. Will you agree to serve me, and be my friend?"

The horse looked over the carnage of the recent ambush, and watched for a moment as my companions made ready to continue marching. "You were last to receive healing. Why?"

I shrugged. "Because it is the right way to do things."

Once again the burning eyes looked right at me. "I will serve you."

I stepped forward to touch his head. "I accept your service, and swear that you will always be treated with justice and affection." I gathered his reins, and led him toward where the others were waiting. "Now, we just need to find you a name."

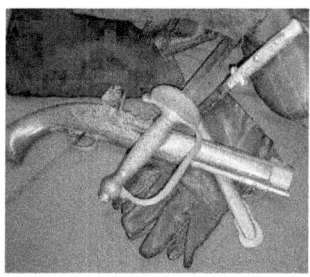

About the Author

P.D. Haynie, known as "Paul" to his face, has been studying the craft of writing since Gerald Ford was President. Along the way, he has allowed himself to be distracted by any and all information that might be useful to a creator of fantasy and science fiction, which is unfortunately almost everything. He lives in Waukegan, Illinois with his wife Julia. He has not actually gone by "P.D." in the real world since shortly after he learned to talk.

Also by P.D. Haynie

Fiddler's Rose, and other books from Spiral Path Publications, are available in print and Kindle/MOBI format from Amazon, in PDF format from DriveThruFiction, and in EPUB format from most e-book vendors.

E-mail spiralpathpublications@.gmail.com for more information!

Fiddler's Rose

Can a dragon sorceress find happiness with a unicorn's ghost?

Love doesn't need to be explicit to engage your heart, and horror doesn't need to be graphic to invade your dreams.

A love story, an epic quest, and a conversation.

www.ingramcontent.com/pod-product-compliance
Lightning Source LLC
Chambersburg PA
CBHW060821120626
46557CB00001B/310